LIST OF WORKS BY OSBERT SITWELL

Fee Fi Fo Fum!

A Book of Fairy Stories

BY

OSBERT SITWELL

LONDON
MACMILLAN & CO LTD
1959

MACMILLAN AND COMPANY LIMITED
London Bombay Calcutta Madras Melbourne

THE MACMILLAN COMPANY OF CANADA LIMITED
Toronto

ST MARTIN'S PRESS INC
New York

PRINTED IN GREAT BRITAIN

AUTHOR'S NOTE

I MUST make acknowledgements to Mr. Leonard Russell, under whose editorship 'Cinderella' appeared in the annual *Saturday Book*, and to Mr. Cyril Connolly, who first presented my 'Dick Whittington' in *Horizon*. Later it was published as a small book by Home and Van Thal, Ltd.

Most of the other stories are retold from nursery versions or from well-known fairy stories, and appear in their present form for the first time. One of them is an invention of my own and I insert it here as a contribution to the body of fairy stories in existence.

O. S.

CONTENTS

CONTENTS

entirely new light on him, may cause his character to blaze genially for you, and to remove him once and for all from the category to which you had consigned him. . . . Let me provide an instance of the sort of thing I mean, taking it from life. . . . There was an octogenarian whom I had known for twenty years and whose company was by most people, including myself, avoided whenever possible because of his interminably long tales of prowess with rod and gun, the fruit of a misspent lifetime devoted to sport : yet one evening he made a remark to me at dinner which revealed an entirely unsuspected aspect of his character and of the very existence of which his acquaintances had hitherto been ignorant. Turning to me, he said suddenly in a low voice, alluding to his other neighbour, whom he had not met before, 'I don't think I like that chap at all. I've got a good mind to give him twenty minutes of my new fishing story after dinner.' Once you had grasped that he regarded the telling of such stories as constituting in effect a private punitive system with its own comparative penalties, he certainly became an entirely new person. . . . Similarly, a fairy story differs with the pen or typewriter of each writer who retells it.

The fairy stories and pantomime stories that follow are not written for — or only for exceptional — children, so much as for their fathers and mothers. But the ferocity and bloodthirstiness of the original stories intended to edify — or at least to interest — very young children resemble in their cruelty those puppet plays calculated to please an identical audience. Take, for instance, *Punch and Judy*, which offers a perfect field for examination. Punch, we are told,[1] descends from Punchinello and, farther back, from Pontius Pilate — though why Pontius Pilate should be made to strangle his infant child, beat his wife to death, and then fling down their two bodies into the street, remains enigmatic. Punch is first, we are informed, arrested by an Officer of the Inquisition, and then put in prison, from which he escapes by means of a golden key. 'The rest is an allegory showing how the lighthearted Punch triumphs over (1) ennui, in the shape of a dog, (2) disease, in the disguise of a doctor, (3) death, . . . and (4) the Devil himself. . . .' Several fascinating larger problems obtrude from this elucidation. Why, for example, should boredom on this occasion assume the form of a dog ? — as a rule human beings, and especially the British, love dogs. And is the embodiment of disease in a doctor intended to be satiric ; near in meaning to a remark that Horace Walpole made in a letter referring to the death of Thomas Gray : that it seemed especially sad that the poet should die from *not* seeing a doctor, the opposite of what killed most people ?

I suppose that fairy stories, in this comparable to nursery rhymes, *can* enshrine various distant historical events, or even prehistoric happenings, or contain allusions to various obsolete religious systems prevailing in the most ancient times ; albeit it would be pedantic, I apprehend, to regard every fairy story as material to be

[1] See Dr. Brewer's *Dictionary of Phrase and Fable*.

Is it too far-fetched to see in the curse laid upon the Princess a likeness between her condition and that of the last Czarevitch, who was liable to die if he cut himself even slightly ; is it too extravagant to think, in connection with this fairy story, of haemophilia — with which he was afflicted, with such incalculable results for the world, and which, before the disease (then known as having 'a skin too few') had been scientifically studied and its symptoms identified, was supposed to be confined in incidence to the Royal Houses of Europe ; is it, then, too conjectural — for it must be admitted that haemophilia is said seldom to attack a woman, although she alone can transmit it — to wonder whether the story of the Sleeping Beauty may not refer to, and arise from, that of some remote but similar prototype ? . . . Or, to take another instance, there is the story of the *Babes in the Wood* which I have also omitted from this collection. In it two orphans — a boy and a girl — have inherited a huge fortune and landed estate which will pass to their uncle and guardian if they die before him. After a year, the wicked uncle hires two ruffians to murder his wards. The assassins, however, fall out ; one kills the other, leaving the children in the wood, where they die during the night and are covered over with leaves by Robin Redbreast. The wicked uncle inherits their possessions, but everything goes wrong with him ; his sons die, his fortune is dissipated. Now, this story occurs in ballad form and was included in Percy's *Reliques* : it also appears in a melodrama of Robert Farrington's in 1599, gifts as an artist in several directions. In addition to playing the violin, he composed music and had written touching threnodies to his mother and to Poppaea. The palace that he had caused to be built — the Golden House — set a new standard for Rome in magnificence and beauty, and in the art of display he was the Max Reinhardt or Diaghilev of his epoch. On the evening in question, no doubt he felt that he had better get on with his practising ; because he was shortly due to give a concert in Athens, where the standard, both of playing and of criticism, remained very high. He would not have formed the habit of working at night, except that people insisted on distracting him during the daytime and, in the middle of some long musical exercise that needed concentration of the highest order, and a great deal of thought and hard work, some slave would be certain to rush in and interrupt him about one thing or another. On this particular occasion he had been at first attracted to the window by the glow : he had never seen the porphyry pillars look so well as they did now in the smoky luminosity of the flames — even more effective than by moonlight ; then admiration had turned to distress and he had wondered what he could do to help. The answer, soon obvious to himself, was *nothing*. . . . Climbing heights gave the Emperor vertigo : so he had played no part nor taken any interest in the A.F.S. Had he joined that organisation, or become its patron, he would only have been in the way. . . . He was — and knew himself to be — as good a violinist as he would be a bad fireman, and he preferred to cultivate his strong rather than his weak points. . . . He had just begun to settle down again to work, when a favourite slave, Diodorus, burst into the Imperial Studio, which commanded a wide view of the burning city, and flinging himself on all fours, lifted up his head to announce at great length the obvious.

'Divine Majesty, it is my duty to bear to you dire tidings !'

'Well, don't go on blathering in such stilted language! Do come to the point. You say you bring me bad news : is that it ?'

'Something too dreadful to relate has occurred. . . . But I feel it would be an abandonment of my sacred task not to break the news.'

'Then tell me, — but first do get up ! Don't lie there prone or crawl about like a tortoise !'

'I don't know how to put it so as to cause your godship least shock.'

'Well, for heaven's sake, make the effort.'

'Divine Majesty . . . Rome Is On Fire !'

'What a nose you have for news ! *You* certainly won't set the Tiber on fire. What on earth do you suppose I thought was happening ? . . . Fireworks ! . . .'

'But the city is burning.'

'Well, what of it ? *I* can't put the fire out, can I ? Leave it to the City Fire Brigade, which is most competent, and don't interrupt me again. Allow me to get on with my music,' the Emperor may well have replied.

Now, that which no doubt shocked the slave, and, after him, the general public, was not so much that the Emperor refused to help put out the flames, though historians pretend it ; no, the accent is on *fiddling*. It was *that* which roused the horror of his subjects.

In the fairy and pantomime stories that I relate here, I have tried in a similar fashion sometimes to state the case from an opposite standpoint. For example, Dick Whittington, observed from the cat's-eye view, becomes quite a different person from the usual hero of what can be described as a typical success story ; and the tale of Cinderella, which I also here present, emphasises other points than those usually dwelt on.

I further consulted the same authority as before on the origin of fairy stories in general. The difficulty was to reach my goal, since the compiler fills the reader's mind on the way with such fascinating items. Who, for example, could resist such entries as the eye has to run through before alighting on *Jack and the Beanstalk* and *Jack the Giant-Killer* ? 'Jack, applied to men, usually in contempt, Cheap Jack, Cousin Jack, Jack Adams, Jack-a-dandy' (the last reference carries a further note, explaining that this term is also rhyming slang for brandy). 'Jack-a-dreams, Jack-a-Lent' — a figure of ridicule similar to Aunt Sally, at which people liked to throw things during Lent — 'a sheepish booby'. Jackanapes, 'a pert, vulgar, apish little fellow ; a prig', said to have been a derisive nickname for William de la Pole, Duke of Suffolk (murdered in 1450), whose badge was the clog and chain of a tame ape. An alternative derivative is also offered as being the 'Jack (monkey) of (imported from) Naples —Jack-a-Napes', 'Jack Brag, Jack-in-the-green, a figure to be found in chimney-sweeps' revels on May Day. . . . Jack Pudding, a buffoon, Jack-sauce, an insolent sauce-box, Jack-snip, Jack-a-lantern, Jack of Newbury, a wealthy clothier in the reign of Henry VIII ; Jack the Ripper, Jack Straw and Jack Ketch, a hangman and executioner, notorious for his barbarity. . . .' Who could refrain from stopping to savour such wayside riches ?

Eventually, however, the reader arrives at his destination and learns that the story of *Jack and the Beanstalk*, which follows, is to be found among people of every climate from Iceland to Zululand ; that the beanstalk is said to be the ash, Yggdrasil, of the Eddas ; that the giant is All-Father ; that his three cherished possessions are a harp — the wind, bagsful of treasure — the rain, and the red hen which laid the golden eggs is to be identified with the sun. Jack himself represents Man, who can make use of these gifts of nature to become rich.

O. S.

an English boy, apple-cheeked, as a rule reliable beyond his years, and given to slouching and sly remarks. A stranger would have guessed him to be a farmer's son, but his father had been a butcher, dead some three years before this story begins. After her husband's death at forty from rheumatic fever, the widow had been obliged to sell the business in order to pay his debts ; nevertheless in later years it was often said of young Jack that in the manner of many great men (*great* was then a term reserved specifically for those who became of a sudden inordinately rich) he owed much to his mother's early training of him, because it had been her habit to din continually into his ears, even when he was a small child, such concise odds and ends of proverbial wisdom as '*Never miss an opportunity*', '*Don't kill the goose that lays the golden eggs*', '*Look after the pennies and the pounds will look after themselves*', and, most often of all, that '*God helps those who help themselves*'. And, indeed, the last and so frequently recurring adage may really have influenced him, for, as will be seen in the course of the next few pages, he helped himself to a good deal at a comparatively early age. The only assets of mother and son to start with were their mutual affection, a thatched cottage, the front of which was thickly covered during the summer with honeysuckle and small red roses, a garden, a meadow, and a cow called Buttercup, which supplied the rich golden butter and creamy milk they sold in the nearest market every morning : sold profitably, because both products looked appetising and abounded in vitamins — albeit these were then called something else.

One day, however, the cow yielded no milk, and in consequence the widow became worried to desperation. Jack tried to find work, but the Trade Union rules forbade it because he was only eleven years of age. Moreover they lived too far away from a town for him to be able to attend a school, and his mother had not been able to give him anything but practical lessons, for she had no letters herself. In consequence, when not employed by her on errands of one sort or another, he spent all of his considerable spare time climbing trees, until he attained an extraordinary proficiency in this art of the youthful, and showed an altogether astonishing agility. This way of spending the hours used, however, to irritate his mother, who frequently would leave her cottage, trace him to a tree-top, and call up to him, 'Why aren't you working? Climbing like that will never get you anywhere!' (Little did she foresee the future.) . . . Soon, his mother was obliged to sell their furniture piece by piece, and even to get what she could for their spare clothing — though of this there was little enough. Finally the day came when with a solemn air she called Jack from the garden and told him to drive Buttercup to market the next morning, and sell her for the best price he could obtain.

On the way there he met an old man with a flowing white beard, who looked, Jack thought, rather like a hermit. He was clad in a long black robe, and wore on his head a high conical black hat decorated with golden suns and stars. . . . Directly the boy was near enough, the stranger spoke to him, saying :

'Good morning, Jack, that's a nice cow you've got. I'd like to buy her.'

'Well, what do you offer, sir ?' asked Jack.

'I'm a wizard, not a merchant or farmer,' replied the old man, 'so I do not buy with money, but I offer you, in exchange for her, five beans. They're not by any means ordinary vegetables, neither broad beans nor scarlet runners ; they are *magic* beans, and if when you reach home you plant them, by morning they'll have grown to the kingdom of the sky.'

Jack, being still young, forgot his mother's careful instructions : the thought of these beans fascinated him, and at once, without any attempt to raise the price, he accepted the offer of the sorcerer ; who then drew out from a deep pocket five small kidney-shaped objects with a hard skin corrugated as a contour map of the world, and counted them into the boy's hand.

Jack started off for home in high spirits, but as he approached the cottage he began to feel a little nervous about his bargain. . . . The widow was waiting for him at the door.

'Well, what have you brought me, son ?' she called.

'I've brought you five magic beans, mother,' he answered.

The poor woman, flabbergasted by her son's un-expected act of disobedience and folly, shouted at him,

'Magic, my foot ! I'll give you beans !' (which is said to be the origin of that well-known slang phrase). She then — for by this time Jack had entered the house — seized the beans from his hand, flung them out of the window, and sent her son straight up to bed without supper.

As Jack lay in the dark room, hungry and cold, and unable for a long time to sleep, he thought of the beans, and determined never to fall into such an error again. It was then that he for the first time comprehended fully the importance of knowing the exact value of all animals and objects, and of money itself. . . . A full moon soon shone into the room, plating the walls with its precious if intangible metal, but this began before long to fall into patches, instead of sheeting a whole surface. He wondered what the reason could be, and for a long time stared at the window, for something appeared in the past hour to be obstructing the entrance of the light, and he also vaguely wondered what could be the curious rustling that he seemed to hear, soft and rhythmic. Though he was not sleepy, he was far too tired physically to get out of bed. If, however, he had been more inquisitive, and had persevered, he would have discovered that the sound was one that no man had ever heard before, or would probably ever hear again ; the sound that trees and plants and all green things make in the process of their growing ; a music usually spread over so long a period, and so slowly, that the human ear cannot catch the pattern of it. He lay there, wondering whether the soft sounds were due to his imagination, until after another half an hour or so he fell asleep.

In the morning he woke up in his familiar room : but the moment his eyes opened, he realised there was a difference ; it was strangely dark. He got out of bed and ran to the window. . . . A beanstalk as thick as the bole of a well-grown oak, only more flimsy in substance, and with leaves as large as those of a great-leaved magnolia, filled the space, casting a green shadow on the white walls. Craning his neck out through the various barriers, he looked upward, and saw there too the curious plant, stretching, apparently for ever, up to the very sky itself. He dressed quickly and, curiosity overcoming his hunger, slipped out before, as he thought, his mother was down, and began with ease to climb the beanstalk. He soon reached the clouds. But he had not passed beyond ear-shot when he heard his mother rush from the cottage, and shout up to him, 'Jack, you come down this instant ! And don't you get it into your head that, after all, it's a magic bean. It's just those hormones you read of.' He was determined not to turn back for anybody, because he wanted to reach the kingdom of the sky, of which the old man had spoken. The top of the beanstalk was level with the clouds, which today were pushed up in fleecy hillocks, and a road led from it to a tall house, grey as the pastures of the angels, and its huge windows shone with reflected light, as though they were the eyes of Gods.

In the doorway, which was as large, the other way

round, as the whole front of his home, stood an enormous woman. Owing to her size, her skin seemed very coarse, and the pores showed like pock-marks, but she had a kind expression, so that Jack, whose exertions had made his appetite all the keener, plucked up his courage to ask her, 'Please, ma'am, could you give me some breakfast ?'

'You're more likely to find yourself part of somebody else's breakfast, if you stay here,' the woman replied, 'for my husband is the celebrated ogre Crunchingbones, and there's nothing he likes so much of a morning as an English boy on toast.'

'Well, I may as well risk being eaten myself, as die of hunger,' Jack answered.

The good-natured woman smiled at this, took him into the tall house, and placed before him bread and cheese and a bowl of milk which Jack soon consumed. Scarcely had he finished when the ground began to tremble with a peculiar rhythm.

'That's *his* footstep,' said the woman ; 'I warned you. He'll be here in a minute.' . . . She seemed terrified at her husband's approach, and lifting Jack up by his collar, threw him into the oven to hide him, and shut the door : but he could peep into the room through a crack invisible on the outside. The sound of gigantic footsteps drew nearer, and in a moment Jack saw the form of a vast man enter the room. He threw down on the table two calves he had been carrying, and said to his wife, 'There's my breakfast : get it ready for me at once !' For some minutes he paced up and down the kitchen — then stopped short and sniffed the air in a most frightening way, like a wild animal. Suddenly he howled out in his ferine voice :

> '*Fee, Fi, Fo, Fum!*
> *I smell the blood of an Englishman!*'

'You're imagining things, dear,' said his wife, 'you don't keep your strength up. You should take more care of yourself.'

'Well, that may be so,' answered the giant, mollified.

In the meantime, while Jack trembled in the oven, Mrs. Crunchingbones had set to, and prepared breakfast for her husband. He ate long and greedily, but the moment he had finished, he dragged from where it stood against the wall opposite him a large chest, unlocked it, lifted the lid, and took out of it two bags. They contained gold coins which he proceeded to count until he fell asleep. Crunchingbones's wife was somewhere at the back of the house, so Jack, creeping out of the oven, seized one of the bags of gold, dropped it into his mother's garden far below, and then swarmed down the beanstalk, home.

At first his mother was angry, for the sack was heavy, and had nearly hit her. 'You careless little beggar, you !' she shouted up at him. 'One of these days, you'll kill someone !' But she softened when she heard his story and saw what the bag contained.

'You acted correctly, Jack,' she commented at the end. 'Fair shares for all ! He has no right to have more gold coins than we !' So she and Jack lived on the ogre's hoard until the last gold coin was spent. After which they existed for some time as best they could, borrowing and running into debt, for their spell of temporary prosperity had debauched them.

At last want of food drove Jack again to explore. The beanstalk still flourished, and he climbed it once more, and once more arrived safely at the ogre's house. Cautiously he entered the kitchen, and, after having made sure that the ogre was out, greeted the wife, saying, 'Hello, Mrs. Crunchingbones, ma'am,' in rather an off-hand manner, as if he saw her every day.

'Hop it, boy !' she replied. 'Wasn't it you that I hid here the very day that my husband missed one of his sacks of gold ?'

'Well,' he answered, 'if I weren't so hungry, I could tell you a few facts about that : they might interest you — but I must eat first.'

The ogre's wife again felt sorry for the boy ; he seemed too young to have much harm in him, and she could see that he was hungry, so she said, 'Sit down over there,' indicating a corner near the oven, and brought him a bowl of milk. He had scarcely finished it when they heard — or, rather, in the first place, felt — the ogre's footsteps approaching. Once more the kind woman threw Jack into the oven, and he was able to watch as before. Once more, the ogre angrily sniffed the air. Once more he bellowed out in his angry, ugly voice :

> '*Fee, Fi, Fo, Fum!*
> *I smell the blood of an Englishman!*'

His wife, however, calmed him, patting him and saying, 'There, there, dear : don't carry on ! You're tired, and will feel better after breakfast' ; and she soon produced three broiled oxen for him.

After he had finished his meal, he shouted sleepily, 'Bring me my hen !'

Accordingly, his wife brought to him a large red hen fluttering and cackling in her arms, put it down and left the room. Crunchingbones commanded 'Lay !' : whereupon the hen cackled again, and laid an egg of gold — which puzzled Jack, for he had always understood from his mother that it was a goose that laid the golden eggs. Indeed, this discovery first began to undermine his mother's authority. However, there was no time to waste, or in which to think this out at the moment, and as soon as the ogre fell asleep and began to snore, Jack crept out of his hiding-place and grabbed the hen. The frightened cackle it put up woke the ogre, but Jack had a good start and was already on his way down the beanstalk before Crunchingbones was out of the house, so that the boy reached home safely with the gold egg in his pocket and the hen under his arm.

The next time Jack climbed his beanstalk it was not from hunger, for the golden eggs procured him and his mother all, and more than all, that they could wish for : no, now Jack wanted to get rich, and easily won treasure had fanned his greed for money. . . . The ogre's house seemed empty, and Jack slunk in without meeting the ogre's wife, and on this occasion for a change concealed

himself in the copper. . . . Soon Crunchingbones returned. Directly he entered, he stopped, sniffed the air,
as he had done on previous occasions, and hitting the
wooden walls with a stick as big as a tree trunk to make
sure that there was no hollow space behind them in
which someone could hide, at the same time bawled out
his theme-song :

> '*Fee, Fi, Fo, Fum!*
> *I smell the blood of an Englishman!*'

At the sound of his voice, his wife hurried in, saying,
'If you really think you do, dear, it will be that little
villain from down below again ; the boy who stole our
gold and our magic hen. If so, he's sure to be in the
oven. That's where he was before, if you remember.'

Jack was terrified that it would be the turn of the
copper next, for he heard Crunchingbones rush towards
the oven, open the door with a bang, and explore it
with great blows from his stick. . . . However, that it
had proved to be empty must have reassured the ogre,
for he did not search the copper, and after his breakfast of
four sheep, roasted, called to his wife : 'Bring me my
harp of gold !' When she had brought it and had left
the room, he commanded : 'Sing, Harp !' and the harp
sang in a golden voice, most touchingly, for more than
half an hour, until the ogre fell asleep. Then the harp
fell silent for fear its singing should wake him.

As soon as the sound of the giant's snoring replaced
its melodious songs, Jack crept noiselessly out of the
copper and grasped the harp : but the moment he

C

touched it, it called out 'Master ! Master !' . . . The
ogre first stirred in his sleep, and then, feeling that
something was amiss, roused himself, and ran to the door
just as Jack was disappearing out of sight down the beanstalk. Crunchingbones looked at the plant doubtfully,
wondering, no doubt, whether in spite of its size it
would support his weight. But from far below the
harp cried again, 'Master ! Master !' and on hearing
this, the ogre threw caution to the winds, and, first
clutching the beanstalk, began to climb clumsily down
it, the whole plant swaying, sagging and drooping under
the unexpected burden.

By this time Jack had reached the ground in safety,
and realising what was happening, called 'Mother,
Mother, bring me an axe !' She hurried out, but was
so startled that she could not move when she saw the
giant's leg protruding out of a cloud as he clumsily felt
for his next foothold. Jack, however, snatched the axe
from her, and wielded it to some purpose, for at the
second blow he cut the stalk clean in two, and the giant
like an avalanche of flesh fell to the ground with a
tremendous crash, making it shake as though an earth-
quake were in progress, and carrying the top of the beanstalk with him : his head was broken, and after a minute
there sounded a death-rattle from him, like a great
hurricane. . . . Now it was to Jack that the harp sang
'Master ! Master !'

In London, and in the provinces too, Jack and his
mother gave concerts regularly for the harp, which

learned to sing Gounod's *Ave Maria*, and made much money for them. Indeed, the house was invariably sold out. With this exceptional musical instrument, and in addition with the hen, as their capital, they started the Golden Egg Bonus Company, a dairy and grocer's shop, combined with a lending library. As Jack could not read, his chief wish — for he affected to despise books, or book-learning, as he termed it — was to get every new offending volume out of the shop as soon as it arrived in it, and this gave an appearance of keenness. The business started in quite a small way : regular customers — those who had spent enough money, without realising that it was too much — were invited to draw a ticket out of a bag, and if it had printed on it a particular number, announced beforehand, the fortunate client found himself awarded an egg of gold. This novel system of bonus continually brought in new and enthusiastic clients, until the smaller competitive shops became deserted and were bought up by the new company. Soon branches of it opened in every large city and prosperous manufacturing town in England and the United States.

Jack and his mother now found themselves in the world of big business, and before long proceeded to sponsor the famous Golden Egg Television and Radio programmes, in which the Golden Harp was a favourite performer. They owned yachts and rented grousemoors in Scotland. But all this work, all this prosperity and luxury, brought their own drawbacks. He never married, and his mother was too old and set in her ways to make an ideal hostess. Moreover, Jack, unable to read, was bored in his leisure hours. His new friends thought him eccentric, for, conscious that the improvement in his circumstances had all followed on climbing a beanstalk, he persisted every day in climbing trees, though he was now of middle age, and guests could not help being surprised when they heard their host hail them from some leafy fastness at the top of oak or chestnut. His mother would try to break him of this habit, but she failed. In fact, he had developed what is now called a fixation. His move to a large mansion in London served to make his eccentricity only more evident. And one morning Lord Beanstalk, as he was now called, for he had lately been created a viscount, was found by the police at the top of an elm, known to be unsafe, in Kensington Gardens. They ordered him to come down, but he refused, and in the ensuing struggle — for ignorant as they were of his identity, they sent up firemen on ladders to capture him — he fell and was killed. His solitary and grieving mother did not long outlive him, and the nationalisation of the Golden Egg Bonus Company that followed.

The Three Jacks
(2) Jack the Giant-Killer

ONCE upon a time — the exact period is uncertain, for though we are told that King Arthur held contemporaneously his mystic and spectral court, yet since that monarch whom we descry so dimly now through the rainbow dust of accumulated centuries is alleged to have reigned for two hundred years, this statement does not help us to identify the precise date or even decade, but we will hazard that it was during that strange historical vacuum of fifty years when the Roman legions had left Britain, and no new invader had yet arrived : that is to say from about A.D. 400 to 450 —, once upon a time, then, when giants still strode across the land, a boy called Jack lived in Cornwall. He was his own master — self-employed, as we say now — and started his career by running a daffodil farm, which prospered, for since the climate was mild, the flowers came out early, and he cultivated new blossoms — for example, he named one after each of the Knights of the Round Table and their ladies — and sent the flowers in damp reed baskets by mule-back at night, in order that the heat of the day should not spoil their perfection, to places so far away as Glastonbury and Tintagel, where they found many buyers. But

soon he wearied of wasting his youth upon the cultiva-
tion of bulbs, and began, after the fashion of many
young men before and after him, to long for a life of
adventure : accordingly he sold his holding, and determined to march across the county to a private battle
with the Colossus of St. Michael's Mount — for Jack
came from the southern coast of the county, and not
from the cloudy promontories and abrupt cliffs of the
north of it. Jack himself was neither tall nor short, was
slim, fair-haired and pleasant-looking. Though he did
not ever realise it, he espoused a popular cause : because
giants were as much abominated by the people of his
era as they have been ever since — today especially —,
and pygmies were even then all the rage. Giants, it was
felt, were out of keeping with the times, were not fly
or spry enough, tended to be cumbersome and to take
up too much room : moreover, usually they had never
been converted to the new religion — in fact, as a body
they belonged to 'the bad old days', a term people then
applied in general to the precedent civilised years of the
Roman Occupation. Also, they were said then to be
apt to brag, and to boast of their strength ; though to us
today this would seem to be more symptomatic of
dwarfish mentality. The giant whom Jack had pledged
to overthrow measured twenty-two feet without sandals,
was broad in proportion and was called Cormoran.
(And here in a long parenthesis we may pause to note
one respect in which giants had the advantage over
dwarfs : both personally and generically, they bore more

resounding and imposing names, equally fine in literature, legend or history. Compare the elephantine trumpeting of such words as Brobdingnagian, Gargantua, Gog and Magog, Goliath, Cyclops, Behemoth, Leviathan, Titan, Queen of Tonga, with the mouse-like squeal of atomy, Lilliputian, midget, chit, Tom Thumb, homunculus, tit, dandiprat and pidwidgeon. Cormoran's name was no exception and augments the total sum of music gigantic, but most delicately, for consider how the addition of a single letter would have altered the force and significance of it : Cormoran*t*, with the fishy association it would inevitably evoke, would have been ridiculous, whereas *Cormoran* possesses a certain nobility of sound, and holds the attention.) Yet even those who have a constitutional bias in favour of giants must nevertheless admit that Cormoran was a *mauvais sujet* — in example, he would from time to time wade across to the mainland, and seize as many hogs, sheep and cows as he could manage —, a mixed-up kid, he would be termed today, but I doubt whether a probation officer, or, indeed, anyone but Jack, could have done much with him.

St. Michael's Mount in that age presented a very different aspect from what it does in ours — only the rock and the treacherous sea round it were the same. On the summit could be seen the remains of a druid temple ; huge monoliths lay on the ground, leaned at grotesque angles or in a few instances still stood upright. The place had a bad reputation ; some said that our giant, who lived in an enormous cave just beneath the top of the Mount, was in reality an emanation from the ruins, which had for centuries before the Romans dismantled the site been the scene of human sacrifices, and others alleged that the giant was in fact a kind of Minotaur in his own Labyrinth. . . . Be this as it may, on the evening with which we are concerned, Cormoran was in his fastness feasting on the viands his last raid had brought him. He sat, naked except for a sheep-skin round his loins, on part of an overturned cromlech in the light of the setting sun, and ate with such an intent desperation — for to keep going such an acreage of body required a continual effort — that he did not notice Jack's arrival on the coast opposite. . . . Jack had taken with him on this expedition a suit of armour (second-best), a pickaxe, a horn and a shovel : he waited for the coming of night, and then, by the light of a full moon, dug a deep pit, such as in those days one prepared for prowling bears, and next proceeded to cover it with branches and green moss, making it look as much like solid earth as possible. When this was done, he flung himself down on the ground between the trap he had made and the sea, and, tired out, fell into a sound, refreshing sleep.

In the early hours of a June day he woke, feeling fit to tackle any giant in the world, and so he dressed and put on his armour. Then, choosing a good tactical position, he took up his horn and blew it very provocatively in the direction of the giant's cave. The sound broke into the dreams of Cormoran, who rushed up to the brow of the Mount in a great rage, and after shaking at Jack, insect-like in his comparative puniness, a huge blue fist — giants often had Reckitts-blue hands : it was a tradition among them, a vestigial survival from the prehistoric days of woad —, responded to the challenge sounded on the horn below, by a blast on a trumpet six foot long. Then, taking it from his lips, he shouted, with his uncouth, animal-like voice,

> '*Go away, you little beast,*
> *Or you will form my morning feast!*'

Jack, when these words reached him, was not frightened so much as interested ; in fact, he rather preened himself, for he comprehended that in a sense the ogre was paying him a kind of compliment ; after all it was not everyone that even a cannibal would *want* to eat. Some of the hermits who lived in caves along the coast owed their immunity, he guessed, as much to the fact that they would plainly make very dry eating as to divine protection, and often it was rumoured that missionaries sent to more savage parts were chosen by the authorities for the same reason. No, obviously, an anthropophagist would prefer someone clean and pleasant to look at. . . . Meanwhile Cormoran had jumped down the side of the Mount, and now taking a step or two towards Jack, fell headlong into the pit. And as he lay there groaning — and his groans were like the sound of a great wind passing through a cavern — Jack took the pickaxe and struck him on the temple with it. Thus did he kill his first giant.

The unexpected fate of Cormoran created a great stir in the neighbourhood. Indeed, Jack received messages of congratulation and presents of flowers and fruit from all over the region : but the news also reached and not unnaturally perturbed the ogre's colleagues and collaborators, who — rightly — foresaw a period of persecution in store for them. Cormoran's kinsman and close friend, the giant Blunderbore, who lived in a grey tower on a rocky promontory lost in the grey-green mists, thick and soft as moss, of the Atlantic coast, was moved to swear publicly that he would avenge his cousin's death, and at the same time assert once and for all the superiority of the race of giants over all others and their exemption from ordinary laws. . . . This particular ogre was nearly forty feet in height, and proceeding to walk south in enormous strides, he came upon Jack in a wood, before that young man had had time even to hear of Blunderbore's oath. The giant took him up in his hand and, stripping him first of his armour, as you may see an ordinary man crack and peel a walnut, splitting and throwing away the shell, then carried him off northward. Jack could only struggle and kick ineffectively in the giant's grip, and they soon arrived at the tower. Here, Blunderbore threw Jack on to the floor of a room, as an ordinary man might throw a cat, and locked the door behind him. The aspect of the chamber was impressive and not at first sight unpleasant. It was — as all the giant's apartments necessarily had to be, or he would have felt cramped — nearly a hundred feet high and seemed to be a kind of grotto, walls, floor and ceiling composed of glittering white shells, of different sizes but of repetitive form — then, suddenly, Jack understood : the room was in reality lined with human skulls and bones, these remains testifying to the number of human beings whom this odious ogre and his repellent cronies had devoured — a discovery which stung Jack into action again, although latterly he had been feeling somewhat stunned by his adventures.

With difficulty he clambered some three score feet up to a window, and contriving to thrust his head between the bars, and taking every precaution not to be observed, looked out. There he saw the vile giant approaching from the distance, with another, who much resembled him, and who evidently, Jack concluded, must be Blunderbore's brother, the no less notorious Slumber-monday ; they were both laughing, and Jack had no doubt that Blunderbore had fetched the newcomer to help to eat him — just the meal for two ogres. . . . In an instant they would reach the tower and it would be too late ; he jumped down, and, seizing a coil of rope he found lying in a corner, climbed up to the window, tied two loops, and skilfully lassoed the giants round the neck as they passed beneath : he then made the rope fast to the bars, and strangled them. Even when the giants were already nearly black in the face, they still continued to bellow like a gale, being clearly amazed at what had happened to them. . . . Jack now managed to break a bar and scramble down the outside wall to the

ground. The first thing he did was to search Blunderbore's body and seize his keys. He then entered the
enormous tower by the main door and went on to
search it thoroughly from top to bottom. . . . There
in a dungeon, seven storeys down, he found three ladies,
who told their rescuer that the giant had condemned
them to die of starvation because they had refused to eat
the flesh of their husbands. . . . In order to encourage
the spirit of aggression in the Little Man, a new law
transferred the goods and property of a dead giant to
the individual or individuals who had killed him ; a
transaction popularly known as Death Duties. Jack
had not wanted St. Michael's Mount — but this tower
was in a different category. . . . So after he had heard
their tale, Jack made the ladies an obeisance, and said
somewhat pompously, with a proprietary wave of the
hand :

'Ladies, as some slight amends for what you have
been through, I offer you Blunderbore Tower, together
with all the treasures it contains, and its gardens, pleas-
ances and lidos.'

Instead of being grateful, however, for his generosity,
one of the three at once undermined his gesture by saying,
'*You*'ve got your head screwed on the right way, young
man, but I wouldn't have the place as a gift. It's too big
for these times.' In the end it proved difficult to get rid
of it at all, and poor Jack found himself very quickly
obliged by his circumstances to hand over his newly
won estate to that private monopoly known as the

National Trust, together with a large sum of money —
larger than he could afford — for its upkeep and that of
the many officials it employed. . . . And even at that,
after the passage of many centuries, little remains of it
today but the memory, so that when on this coast the
wind howls horribly at night, the wives of the local
fishermen administer cold comfort to whining children,
by saying to them : 'Hark ! There's Blunderbore and
his terrible brother yelling for you for their supper !'

After resting for a year, Jack, who was beginning to
regard himself as the champion of the Little Man against
the oppression of the over-life-size, made a journey to
Wales in search of another giant to slay. He walked for
many days, passing through the holy city of Glastonbury
— where King Arthur was at the moment holding
council —, from there to Bath, a resort already sadly
fallen from its pristine Roman splendour, but with, still
living in it, a few old ladies who were the daughters of
former Roman officers or civil servants, and who had
either chosen, or been compelled by events, to remain
in Britain ; then on to Bristol and the Severn Valley,
until at last he reached the forests, mountains and moors
of Wales. When he arrived in that strange and lovely
country, he sought in vain at first for somewhere to
spend the night. For many miles he proceeded without
passing a single human habitation, but, just as dusk was
falling, he came to the postern of a large castle, built of
little stones. He was about to knock and beg shelter for
the night, when rather to his dismay, a giant — for even

by the failing light, the immense size of head and shoulders
was evident — looked out of a window high up in the
wall, and called down to him, 'Like to stay here the
night, sonnie?' Jack gratefully accepted, for he was
very tired, and after all, he reflected, there must be good
giants and bad giants : it was not fair to tar them all
with the same brush. But as he was meditating in this
vein, he heard the giant — whose name was Williams —
call down to the cook, 'Send word to the butcher that
I shall not need the two calves I ordered for tomorrow.'
That this cancellation should synchronise with his unexpected visit struck Jack as rather too much of a co-
incidence — but surely even an ogre would not be so
obvious.

The young man was shown into a comfortable bedroom : but though he undressed, went to bed, and fell
asleep almost at once, he cannot at heart have felt wholly
at ease, for he was not surprised to find himself suddenly
wide awake. The giant was evidently striding up and
down in the next room — for him, stealthily — and was
repeating to himself the couplet (it is to be noticed how
giants, rather than use ordinary speech, prefer whenever
possible to lisp — no, to bellow rather than to lisp — in
numbers) :

> 'Jack will not live to see another sun :
> My club will find him, and his blood shall run!'

Now — as he feared, all too late — innocent Jack comprehended his danger. Not an instant was to be lost, if
he were to save himself, so he leapt out of bed, and look-

ing round by the light of the moon, seized a very large log of firewood, almost the size of the trunk of a tree, and substituted it for his body, in the hollow his lying there had made in the bed. He then hid in a cupboard and held his breath. Before three minutes had passed, he heard the giant tiptoe to the door, open it, and then he saw through a crack the huge figure approach the bed, and aim blow after blow, heavy enough to fell a steam-roller, at the form he thought he could distinguish there. So sure was he of his quarry that he was not even undeceived by the wooden percussion the log gave out when beaten, and he left the room singing to himself the lines :

'No more a stranger lies behind the door ;
His bones will soon be underneath the floor.'

Early next morning Jack knocked at Williams's door, and entered without being bidden. The giant was still snoring, with a sound like that of a cathedral organist playing *Lohengrin*. He stirred as Jack came towards him, and then sat up, the movement of his body resembling a cosmic disturbance — more especially as he trembled, because at first, till Jack spoke, he thought his visitor to be a ghost. Thus confronted by his next meal, as it were, and before he could get a word out, he heard Jack say to him politely, 'I have come, sir, to thank you for your gracious hospitality.' Perceiving by these words that his intended victim was still flesh and blood, the giant made an effort at self-control, but was nevertheless so startled that he forgot to use rhyme, and spoke quite simply, rather in the manner of a doctor who, after attending a patient for several days, is naturally astonished to find him still alive :

'And how are we, this morning ; did we sleep well or were we disturbed by anything ?'

In reply, Jack showed his composure by himself indulging, for a change, in the giants' habit of rhyme :

> '*I dreamt a huge rat planned to kill ;*
> *What saved me was my ear and skill.*'

The giant looked both furious and puzzled.

At breakfast, Williams offered his guest his own bowl, saying :

'Have some hasty pudding, Jack ?'

'Some *nasty* pudding ?' echoed Jack, who had misheard. 'You don't make it sound very attractive.'

The giant, in reality very annoyed at the insult, ostensibly was content merely to correct his guest.

Jack accepted the giant's huge bowl, for he had contrived to secrete a leather bag over his stomach, so now he could hide in it the nauseous concoction offered him. . . . Then, facing the giant, as if to challenge him — for he knew that giants were vain, while he shared as well the English view that the Welsh are apt to be boastful —, he said, 'I'll show you a fine trick, sir,' and taking out a knife, ripped open his coat and bag, so that the hasty pudding spilt on the ground.

The stupid Williams did not perceive the deception and, determined to prove that in no respect was Jack his superior, snatched the knife from Jack, plunged it into his own stomach and, with a roar like that of a multitude of lions, fell dead.

Encouraged by his victories and the increasing fame they brought him — crowds flocked to see him, and he continually received messages asking him to contribute a highly paid account of his feats to one of the popular monkish chronicles of the day (nor did he like to explain in reply that he was scarcely able to read or write, for he had never shown a turn for letters), Jack now prepared to embark on a regular crusade against giants. With this purpose in view, he bought a horse — a strawberry roan, the colour of which caught his fancy — and further purchased some other invaluable aids to the cause he had at heart : a cap of knowledge, a sword of sharpness, and an elegant coat which made him invisible when he put it on : (this last proved useful, not only with giants, but to guard him against mobbing by the vast numbers of his supporters). . . . On his next expedition he rode north for several days without meeting on the way a single giant. No sooner, however, had he entered Sherwood Forest, than in a grove of oak trees he perceived a giant dragging with each hand behind him, along the ground by their golden hair, a knight and his lady. Jack hit the giant as hard as he could — but he did not find it easy to reach the upper part of the monster's body, for Habberjam — this proved to be his name — was twenty-eight feet and some odd inches tall, and though Jack had slain taller, each case presented its own problem. This attack caused Habberjam to drop his

D

captives, in order to take a swipe back at the impudent
midget, for as such the aggressor appeared to him : but
Jack quickly slipped on his precious coat, so that the
giant, roaring in his onrush : 'Hit someone your own
size ! I'll teach you !', found himself obliged to lunge
at what had become empty air, overreached himself, and
toppling over, like a tower falling, lay prone on the
ground. His opponent at once jumped on his back, and
drawing his new sword, plunged it between the ogre's
ribs and killed him. Jack then took off his coat and made
himself visible again.

The knight, who was brushing the dust from his
armour — he had lost his vizor —, offered Jack a large
reward if he could find the giant's stronghold, and his
lady said to him, 'I don't know what I can do to thank
you, except let down the rest of my hair' ; upon which
she undid a braid, and her long golden mane cascaded
down her back, and from it tumbled numerous gold
coins, running on their sides along the flat ground of the
glade with the abruptness of their fall. She told Jack,
further, to keep all the coins he could find. After he
had picked up as many as he could see, he proceeded on
his way, searching, as the knight had exhorted him, for
the den of the dead ogre. . . . He had not gone far
when a giant stepped out of a cavern of two storeys in a
hillside : he did not see Jack, for his eyes were searching
the country below as if he were looking for someone.
Jack knew him at once by his repulsive likeness to the
dead Habberjam : this must be his brother, Trumple-

skull, waiting for Habberjam to return, and the cave (full
of bones, he noted) must be the giants' duplex lair. He
at once dismounted, pulled on his coat, attacked Trumple-
skull, killed him, cut his head off, and carried it back to
the forest grove, where he claimed and obtained the
reward the knight had offered.

The following morning Jack set out again. After a
ride of many days, with few events to record, through
the dales and through the woods that seemed very silent
and curiously empty, except for the smell of honeysuckle
and sweetbriar penetrating through the green glow of
sunlight on countless leaves, Jack met a hermit, who had
by some means or other heard that he was in the neighbourhood. The white-bearded old man, dressed in rags
— he would now be called a tramp or hobo —, came out
of the cave he had scooped for himself within the Roman
Wall, and then asked politely, 'Might you be Jack the
Giant-Killer, sir?' (This was the first time Jack had been
so addressed, and he felt flattered.) When Jack affirmed
his identity, the anchorite led him through a gap in the
Wall, and pointing at a distant hill to the north, said,
'On the top of yon hill lives the giant Galligantus,
attended by his abominable crony, Starmint the Sorcerer.
They inhabit an enchanted castle : but you can never
see it. Its halls are full of translated human beings ;
among them, the Duke of Glastonbury's daughter, whom
they kidnapped and brought here, far from her home,
and turned into a doe. Swear to kill the two villains. . . .
Take care of yourself, run no risks that you can avoid,

and remember always that Galligantus is thirty-eight foot high, and prodigiously powerful.'

On the skull of a saint with which the old man's habitation was furnished, Jack pledged his word to the hermit to destroy the two miscreants, and at once rode off in the direction of the hill. As he drew nearer, it began to present the dimensions of a mountain, and soon he and his horse started to climb. Hour after hour he persevered, until he reached the cloud which always so completely hid the castle : but once he had penetrated this vaporous camouflage and defence, invented by Starmint, the whole vast, ancient building stood brilliantly illuminated by the sun. Jack stopped a moment, tethered his horse in the circumambient cloud, and donned once again his jacket of invisibility ; so he was able to slip between the two guardian griffins, whose wings were composed of the finest feathers of fire, without their noticing him. The castle walls resembled cliffs, they seemed to be all of one stone, without mortar, and they were crowned with tower after tower of different heights and with countless turrets, shaped like helmets. On the main gate hung from a nail a golden trumpet, and under it was inscribed the notice — plainly by the ogre himself, for it was in rhyme, and the letters of which the words were composed stood each at least a foot high —

The mortal who can place this to his lips
Will cause a powerful giant's eclipse.

Jack contrived to read this declaration, though at first he stumbled over some of the words. The trumpet was fastened well above his reach, but holding the sword of sharpness in his invisible right hand, he jumped in the air, and at his third attempt, dislodged the instrument. He then, in spite of its weight, lifted it to his mouth and blew a resounding call. When the echo had died down, he could hear the answering cries of animals of several sorts from tower and dungeon. As these sounds also faded, the great gates flew open of themselves, and our hero entered to find Galligantus and Starmint in a corner of the Vaulted Hall, cowering, because they knew by the brazen challenge offered them that their evil reign was over and their end near. The shivering of the giant in his sudden panic was so violent as to make the stout walls tremble. He did not attempt to defend himself, for he could not see his assailant. Jack climbed up on the ridges of Galligantus's armour, and stabbed him through the temple. Quietly he crumpled up, and Jack slid off him on to the floor. Meanwhile the sorcerer was protesting his innocence to the empty air, spinning round continually to face a new quarter, for fear that Jack should materialise there and attack him, and making a thousand casuistical excuses. His narrow, pointed features were contorted with terror when he saw the giant fall to the ground. From innumerable cellars the lowing and barking and bleating mounted to an agonised crescendo, for a feeling of excitement invested everyone and everything. The magician tried to explain these sounds, too, saying, 'Good sir, I cannot see you, but let me introduce myself. I am the scientist, Starmint. The

There he related the whole story to that monarch : who at once commanded him to go back, taking with him a royal seal as token of authenticity, and bid the Duke of Glastonbury's daughter to give her hand in marriage to Jack. Further, the Sovereign created him a knight in the next Birthday Honours, and bestowed upon him other lands besides those, including Galligantus's mountain, which he had automatically acquired by his dispatch of the ogre. Finally, in addition, the King gave Jack and his heirs the right to bear for ever on the family coat-of-arms the head of a giant.

The Three Jacks
(3) Jack the Shark-Killer

THE third Jack was an American, in appearance typical
of his epoch, with crew-cut hair and well-defined
features, — but he was myopic, his only physical misfortune. He lived in New Stamboul on the ocean coast
of Florida, that mainland annexe to the islands of the
West Indies, offering in place of towering cliffs and great
vertiginous mountains a flat land of sub-tropical scrub,
of white sand and of dark, thorny bushes in the process
of being translated into orange groves. Here the sea
was everywhere more important, more full of light and
colour, than the land ; which in its turn owed its effects
less to its own skeletal formation than to the sculpturing
light. Certainly Jack himself was more at home in salt
water than on the land, because from the age of sixteen
he had been celebrated throughout the State for his
prowess in diving and swimming, even more than for
his dancing. But he was not content ; he desired wealth
as well as recognition, and so far riches had eluded him.
He longed, as do many of the simple, to have his hours
pinned down, so that each day could be set out in the
same way that the old-fashioned entomologist used to
set out the wings of a dead butterfly. He pined, too, for

the sempiternal gaieties of great cities. . . . Yet on the morning in question, as he strolled down to the deserted beach — Florida in June was almost free of visitors —, how little did he expect to achieve so immediately, through a chain of circumstances that would be set in motion within an hour by his bathing, his other ambition, to command a fortune. . . . He was in a good mood since he was immensely looking forward to a party. New Stamboul could be very dull when it reverted to a small out-of-season sub-tropical town with few festivities, but tonight there was to be a Charity Ball and the committee had asked him to open it by giving an exhibition dance with a partner he was asked to select for himself, but had not as yet chosen.

Arriving at the beach, he first surveyed the scene. . . . The prospect was empty except for pelicans which as usual were dropping into the sea with a sudden and substantial plomp, a flopping sound as if a brown-paper parcel had hit the water ; and he noticed that, far out, the rolling breakers appeared to be larger and nearer together than usual. Then, after removing his spectacles and replacing them with swimming-goggles, he presently took off his dressing-gown and clutching the spear he always carried in case he should come upon a big fish, proceeded to advance into the water and swim as far as where the breakers began to bear crests of white. . . . Reaching there at first he splashed about, seized by the invigorating enchantment of salt water and fresh air. Then all at once he realised that the sea was not so empty this morning as he had thought ; a face smiled cosily at him from the next wave, quite near. In return he gave an answering smile of pretended recognition. Though he could not be certain who it was — it must be, he decided, one of his friends from New York or Chicago. For a while he kicked about on the top of his wave. The face certainly reminded him of someone and he tried to identify it — then he turned round and saw the smile opposite him expand into a voracious and cynical grin : at last he comprehended. It was a shark ! For a moment he almost sank from terror — and from surprise, for sharks never approached so near the shore as this. However, he recovered himself instantly, brought to his senses by the magnitude and urgency of his danger, and began again to splash wildly : and in those few seconds as many thoughts and scenes passed through his mind as are said to return to a man drowning.

He recalled, for example, reading a year or two before a description of marine life in mid-Pacific written, if his memory was not at fault, by Thor Heyerdahl. The adventurous author of *The Kon-Tiki Expedition* pronounced that sharks were not by nature cruel, but were the victims of their emotions. This monster, notwithstanding, — the smile, he noted, seemed a little nearer — appeared to be in no need of psycho-analytic help but was plainly a fine and large specimen of the blue shark, about twenty feet long, and possessed of a purpose — and one purpose only. His intentions he now made clear by a hungry snapping of his jaws. What, Jack wondered, could he do to defeat this obvious killer ? He recollected, too, some facts acquired from one of those magazines which process information into a concentrated form and which in America often provide the serious reading matter of the earnest-minded young. The writer had pronounced that sharks were timid — or at least cautious — and could be driven off if you knew how to do it. If Jack were to try to swim away, he realised he would be no match for the shark, which would pursue him and probably deprive him of both legs at the first bite. Therefore the only method to offer a chance of survival was directly to attack the gigantic fish and to kick about and make as much noise as possible. (Indeed, the reason that he was still alive, he concluded, must be because he had been idly but vigorously splashing about on the top of the waves.) If only he could get near enough to use his spear, he might be able to drive off his opponent. He also remembered reading about the unpleasant and corrupt *milieu* of a shark ; that he was always attended by one or two pilot-fish, who escort their master to his feeding ground, receiving tit-bits in reward, so he must take precautions not to become involved with them as well, and he recollected, further, that a shark acts as host to the remora, or shark-sucker, a parasite which clamps itself to the body of the shark. . . . Why, even at this moment the top of one was visible riding above the water like the periscope of a submarine. . . . Jack now acted with rapidity. Suddenly and with all his force he attacked the creature and showed as well as courage a certain resource and ingenuity, pricking and piercing the fish's lean and streamlined sides until his perturbation persuaded him to see enemies where there were none and to lash out at the imaginary host with his tail and snap his jaws until, as the water round broke into explosions of grey and white, even his own splashing about began to frighten the shark. It was, of course, a risky game to play, because Jack had no advantage over his ferocious and gigantic foe except the great disparity in their size, which enabled the young man to move and turn more rapidly. But though he had in the space of a few minutes a score of improbable escapes, he persisted in his tactics until at last one of the blows that Jack aimed at his adversary produced bleeding, and the sight of this incarnadination of the surrounding sea must have terrified the shark, for he made off at high speed. . . . Jack must, he realised, have hurt the monster more than he knew at the moment of striking, since he became aware of an immense watery tumult in the direction in which the shark had disappeared, followed by absolute silence. . . . Could he, he wondered, by a lucky chance have killed the enormous fish ? He did not consider it likely, nor did he care much, for in any case he had proved himself the victor.

As Jack swam out of the space of discoloration towards the shore he could hardly believe that he was safe once more : but he felt utterly exhausted and as he rested for a little, floating again on the surface of the water, it seemed to him that he experienced a new sensation as of some heavy weight pressing on his shoulder, together with a kind of numb dull pain. Tentatively, in the meantime treading water, he investigated, probing the place. He touched a slippery, slimy surface and at once understood ; the remora must at some crucial point in the struggle have detached itself from the shark's back, and fixed itself instead on Jack's shoulder in token of transferred allegiance to the winning side. '*Le Roi est mort. Vive le Roi !*' It was a nuisance, he reflected as he swam, a very great nuisance : on the beach it might look in keeping and impart an extra touch of local colour, but at any social gathering it would seem ridiculous to enter a room with a fish on his shoulder, either exposed through a hole in his white dinner-jacket, or so smothered over by clothes that Jack would seem a hunchback ; for instance, that very night at New Stamboul — which reminded him he had as yet found no partner. . . . At this point, when he had nearly reached the shore, he looked round and discovered just behind him another swimmer, Mr. Macbabble, the father of Dorinda, the very girl he had intended to invite to be his dancing partner tonight ! Though he only knew him slightly, he recognised him. . . . It was strange, Jack thought, that he hadn't noticed him in the water before. When the newcomer drew nearer, the remora gave a painful jerk to Jack's shoulder, as if in order to call the attention of his mount to the new arrival. Mr. Macbabble, who was now climbing out of the water, approached and called out cheerfully :

'Good morning, Jack. You've saved my life.' All the same he did not look in too good trim. Indeed, he appeared to be very battered and was bleeding profusely.

'A shark was attacking me,' he continued, 'but it made off when it saw you. How can I ever reward you?' But here he paused and directed a glance of strong moral disapprobation at the remora, now reared up to its full height.

Jack was practical by nature and at once put forward his claim.

'By letting Dorinda open the Charity Ball as my dancing partner, tonight,' he replied immediately. 'I've been asked——'

'What's it in aid of?' her father interrupted, rather rudely.

Jack told him, and the older man said, 'All right, but you must get rid of your remora first. I can't allow my daughter to be seen with you in public if you insist on going bogussing about the place with a fish on your shoulder.' And suddenly he gave the creature, who, Jack thought, seemed somehow to recognise the new arrival, a vicious tug, but the remora resisted and Mr. Macbabble pretended not to notice it further, though he added to Jack under his breath, 'I'll get rid of it for you for good in a minute or two.' He continued to talk for a little while about the ball — then unexpectedly hurled himself on the remora, and dragged and smacked the creature until he had dislodged it. As it lay on the ground he gave it a final kick, then picking it up, cast it into the sea. . . . Mr. Macbabble now reverted to his story of the shark attacking him : the cuts in many parts of his body, he said, had been caused by the shark's teeth, but would soon heal. The whole story, however, sounded in some way dubious, Jack thought, but even as the two men talked, the wounds began to heal with astonishing rapidity, as if touched by a magic wand.

'Dine with us tonight,' Mr. Macbabble said, 'but come and have a cocktail with me first, and I'll tell you the true story if you promise not to divulge it to anyone else. Besides, you've never seen our little home here. Gee, I shall be glad to be back in it again.'

That evening Jack arrived in good time at the financier's house. He was shown straight into a room with a bar ; behind which stood Mr. Macbabble busily engaged in stirring dry martinis in a glass jug. After his third cocktail, Mr. Macbabble observed, 'Well, I had better confess the truth, strange as it is. I shall feel better if I tell someone. . . . You are acquainted with me only slightly, but at least you know who and what I am, a business man, a financier, — yes, and, of course, a philanthropist. Through my efforts millions of people have found their lives changed. I corner wheat in one country, meat in another, and out of the large profits I make, much goes to the alleviation of the ills my energy has created elsewhere. I support many enterprises and I carry on my shoulders a shoal of human remoras. . . . Well, while in New York, I had brought off a particularly happy deal, by which, however, I accidentally impoverished my associate in many previous financial adventures, George Godalming. Now his wife is a witch, as you have probably heard.

'Well, when I arrived here a few days later, the first person I ran into was this hag whom I had thought to be in New York. She looked at me and said : "You've ruined your old friend, my husband. Now we must have a little talk. . . . Don't try to get away or you will have further cause to regret your actions. You're nothing but a shark ! But this time you're going to suffer for it. . . . Swim under your true colours, be faithful to your nature and remain a shark until at last you're killed by a young man with a spear, and find yourself a man again !" . . . She then muttered a few rhythmical sentences in some barbarous guttural lingo, and even while the words were still on her lips, I found myself a wereshark finning my way through deep waters, and I could not help noticing that as they sensed my presence all smaller fish sped away. . . . For a month now I have been a blue shark and I never want to be one again, even for an hour, — though almost the worst part of it was being obliged to carry on my back that treacherous and supercilious fish.

'Now we'll go and join my daughter, who is tonight to be your partner at the ball. She's the sole heiress of my fortune — as well as very probably the fortunes of most of those with whom I collaborate.'

Everything, Jack noted, was the acme of good taste. There was a library, for example, with no books in it so that it could not get dusty. . . . Macbabble led Jack through a Spanish gallery into an enormous hall. In front of each wall was a line of suits of armour standing up in begging positions, such as a hungry French poodle assumes, alternating with stuffed bears holding trays. One suit of armour had been fitted for radio. . . . There, alone in the middle of the room, sat Dorinda, in a functional chair made of steel rods on which was slung a square fragment of zebra skin. She looked very lonely sitting all by herself in that huge hall, but even prettier, Jack thought, than on the other occasions when he had met her. Her fair skin seemed to glow and her hair to glisten. Before the night was out he had fallen in love with her. The exhibition waltz with which they opened the ball was a great success — but, indeed, the whole evening was so to him — and it was only the first of many such evenings that they were to spend together. For within a month Jack had married Dorinda and they lived happily ever afterwards in the odour of great wealth.

E

Cinderella

CINDERELLA was really a pretty girl — when you could see her : her hair, and her complexion especially, seemed to proclaim a warmth of blood and love of life, and her foot was so small that all other girls were jealous : *when you could see her*, I write, for generally, as now, she was the spinning, invisible centre of a whirlwind of dust. As her stepsisters reached the first landing, and saw raging in front of them that storm of particles, the elder, Pamela, remarked to the younger, 'So *that's* where she is !' and called into it :

'Cinderella, dearest, do stop dusting and come and talk to us about the ball tomorrow. We've both of us determined to take you to it, even if we have to drag you there. But all this dust is bad for your skin. It coats. . . . Well, as it happened, I passed a hoarding which still carried the poster we used to see everywhere during the last election — and which they said at the time won it. You remember the slogans. *"Dare to Be a Woman and Vote for National Skin Food." "After Housework Socialise Your Complexion."* So I suddenly thought of you and went straight to the Ministry of Physical Culture's Beauty Parlour, and got you a pot of Welfare Face Cream.' Here she held up a round glass jar in her hand. 'But you'll have to lie down all tomorrow morning,' she continued, 'and pat it into the skin gently with the tips of your fingers.'

The cloud still continued to spin lightly but suffocatingly on its axis, and caused Diana, the younger sister, to sneeze. Pamela said softly to her :

'Darling, see what you can do. Perhaps you'll be more successful !'

Diana blew her nose and called :

'Cinderella, Cinderella, where are you ? I can't even see you. Do stop dusting and come and talk to us instead. After all, there is so little entertaining nowadays, and the ball is sure to be a lovely sight. All the older women will be wearing their jewels, and I've never even seen them. You can't go on dusting the *whole* time. Half an hour with the Dustette we gave you would do all this work that takes you such hours.'

A sound of crying issued from the centre of the spinning motes, and a small-girl voice whined :

'You're always insinuating something, you two ! When you gave me the Dustette, you told me you'd got it to help me. . . . But *now* I understand. It's because you think I don't dust thoroughly, and that a machine would do it better. I work my fingers to the very bone for you, and that's all the reward I get. How can I come to the ball, when I have to clean the whole house for you ?'

Pamela and Diana walked on upstairs disconsolately. One said to the other :

'There's nothing to be done ! And she can be so charming if she wants ! It's an absolute mania — what they call a complex, I suppose. . . . Never mind, she can't help it, poor child ! Mama told me that 'Rella's mother had been just like that, too.'

Here we must break off to talk a little of that lamented lady, because it had indeed been from her mother that Cinderella had learned the virtues of resignation, and from her example that she had deduced the power it gave you over ordinary people. Ever since Cinderella could remember, she had felt a special devotion for her mother, and for her maternal grandfather, the Bishop ; had dwelt in her own mind on how unselfish they were, and had determined to grow up to resemble them. Sometimes when, as a small child, the thought of their goodness filled her head, she would take the sweet she was sucking out of her mouth and fling it away : though the performing of this act of abnegation caused her to sob, scream and hold her breath for hours and thus induced severe headaches in all those round her. Humpleby, her nurse, who had been nursery maid in the Bishop's Palace, used, after she had put the child to bed, to say to a friend who came to see her :

'Thankful I am to have half an hour and a bit of cheese to myself at last. Miss Cinderella's been a regular little Atrocity Story all day long : throwing her sweets away and fair roaring, just like her dear mother before her. It's in the blood.'

Cinderella had not only learned how — or, to be more precise, in what manner — to be good, but also how to manage a house, from her mother : who, ever since she had married, had defiantly refused to consider herself. Indeed, her very first act on arriving home after her honeymoon had been to discharge the two old servants who had looked after her husband and his parents before him, and to shoulder all their work herself.

'*We* can't afford it,' she had said, 'and the nation can't, either ! The man-hours they waste here would be better employed in a factory. . . . In these days,' she would add, for in the frenzy of her virtue and patriotism her phraseology — as is often the case — would tend to grow a little muddled, 'in these grave days, every man, and every woman, too, must put his hand into the till, and then we shall win through.'

When Cinderella had been born, her mother had engaged old Humpleby. Otherwise she employed no servants, only a help. (I repeat, a help !) The mistress of the house as a rule refused to take nourishment of any sort — at least in the presence of her husband : though he sometimes observed tea and toast being rushed up to her bedroom, as if for first aid, by Humpleby. But this did not count as food. The consumer herself made this clear by the way in which she ignored it, complaining :

'I have no time to eat. I leave it to others with plenty of time on their hands.' Here she would stop speaking, in order to dart a look of disapprobation at her husband, and then resume, 'Let others — it is not for me to judge

or name — let others, I say, who like it, indulge their
gross appetites. I think the hours can be better employed. Come, Cinderella ! Let us start our work. It
will soon be Spring Cleaning Time.' And with a
sweeping rustle of reproach, she would leave the room,
adding to Cinderella, in that voice in which no doubt all
trade secrets are imparted : 'First we must pile up all the
furniture under dust-sheets in the middle of each room,
in case someone should come in and sit down.'

From her mother, Cinderella had received, too,
lessons of a more practical and direct nature. . . . For
instance, when Cinderella's father, whom long-standing
but unformulated accusations had made timid, ventured
to eat at home, her mother would not, of course, join
him at his meal, but would dust outside the dining-room
in a manner that gave full vent to her feelings. She
would rap the furniture sharply with the back of her
brush, and send avenging spirals of dust that had lain
quietly in corners for months to penetrate under the
door and through the keyholes until his own sneezes
obliged the poor husband to acknowledge his conscious-
ness of his wife's lurking but virtuous presence outside.
Thus it had been through continual quiet observation of
her mother that Cinderella had in time come to comprehend that dusting was not to be deemed merely a
form of housework, but constituted in able hands a form
of self-expression, rather like — though also very unlike
— the art of using the fan in Nippon : so that each flick
with a duster, each tap with a brush, each fall, each

breakage could be made to proclaim throughout the house the mood of a great executant. . . . Of course, the lesson was never explicit : her mother never said :

'Darling, if you ever want specially to harass your father, this is the way to dust.'

No : she would approach it more after this fashion :

'Daughter mine, housemaids are careless. You will, even if you could find them, do better without them. They never set about things properly. . . . Now, supposing your father is shut up in his study working, and you haven't seen him all the morning, and don't like to ask him to go into another room while you dust, this is the best way to proceed.'

Her mother showed her, too, just how to nick the china — for Sèvres and eighteenth-century German porcelains, of which he was an acknowledged connoisseur, were among the gross appetites which her father indulged —, thereby removing from the object at one delicate and expert rap, both all the esthetic pleasure to be derived from it, and all financial value. And one morning, when they were alone, her mother did impart one of her secrets directly, by word of mouth.

'Let me give you a hint that your dear old godmother gave me before my marriage. Never, dearest 'Rella, when you have smashed one of your father's things, *never* tell him all at once. Mince matters. Break the news as well as the china' — and here she gave one of her rare but merry laughs — 'Come up to him affectionately and say something like this. "Daddy, darling,

I've something awful to confess . . . the most dreadful thing that has ever happened in this house. I can't bring myself to tell you. . . . Something fearful. Oh, I can't say." Go on like that for a little, watch him until his eyes begin to bulge from their sockets, and then let him have it straight ! You'll find he'll almost be relieved. But remember, if it's a valuable thing you've destroyed, to remind him also that you've saved him the wages of a housemaid. That always produces good results, too.'

As the reader may imagine, Cinderella became a proficient pupil, and soon, at a very early age, there was no treat to which she so ardently looked forward as the promise of being allowed to stay at home and do a few hours' good dusting with her mother. As for Spring Cleaning, the thought of it lit her days, a beacon shining, as Christmas gleams ahead for other children.

Alas, when Cinderella was fifteen her mother fell ill and died of premature virtue. *Passed away*, which was the phrase most commonly used of her, hardly did justice to the fiery resignation and assertive selflessness of her departure from this earthly scene. Her farewell to her husband, whom she sustained with the promise that she would meet him and accompany him throughout eternity, was long cherished and pondered by him. And her daughter never forgot the last words the sainted woman spoke. They were alone.

'Cinderella! Always remember your poor mother, murdered by hard work and neglect. For her sake, stay at home and look after your father, even if he pretends that he wishes you to go out. Learn to be a helpmate !'

After which words, plainly spoken, the poor lady turned on her side, and with one final sigh allowed her soul to take wing.

Thus it had been that Cinderella, while still young in years, had donned the mantle of dust handed on to her by her mother. It was extraordinary, old friends of that lady would tell one another, 'how suffering had brought the child out'. In her ways she seemed more like a woman of thirty than a girl who had not yet reached sixteen. Her days were full. As her mother had done before her, she managed the whole house : but she substituted scorpions for her mother's whips. After preparing and cooking her father's meals, she would serve them herself, dusting outside in the interval. While handing him a dish, she would sometimes further aggravate its taste by telling him of the manner in which it was concocted, and listing its ingredients. The food was by no means plain. She put imagination into it.

'This is only an experiment,' she would begin, as she offered him a sweet. 'It's one of the new recipes broadcast by the Ministry of Food from all stations for Hardship Week — menus called *Dainty Dishes for Dull Days*. I thought this one might appeal to you. It's quite simple, rather like that pudding Mumsie used to make. I'll read it to you. "Take a tin of rhubarb — preferably one that *needs* opening —, shred the contents and flavour with cloves and cinnamon, and lay at bottom of dish, which may be washed first. Add a thin layer of sponge, and some remnants of an old jar of marmalade (marmalade essence will do, if you have finished the pot). Then take an ounce of powdered egg, beat up with a little condensed milk, pour on top and dust with pink peppermint powder and decorate with dice of old toast soaked in treacle. Some cooks also introduce a pretty touch by sprinkling with cochineal : if this cannot be obtained, there are plenty of good home-grown insect substitutes. Sweeten according to taste with saccharine, and serve tepid." . . . It's quite original, I think. . . . "Something different." . . . But I haven't the time to give to the cooking I should like to have — if I had, I believe I could turn you out some real surprises, Daddy. . . . As it is, in a large old house like this, there's always something to be done without having to look for it.' And she began to cry.

Cinderella's father, in spite of the indigestion from which he suffered chronically, never failed to be moved by the sound of his daughter's grief.

'You must not work so hard, my darling,' he would say, after trying to swallow a mouthful of the sweet. 'You're becoming morbid. You should go out more. Fresh air will soon make things seem easier.'

'How can I go out,' she would retort, 'when I haven't even begun to blacklead the grates yet, let alone clean the lamps ?'

'That reminds me,' her father went on, 'I mean to have electric light put in this winter — I've already got

92 out of the 108 permits necessary. It'll give you more leisure.'

'Well, if you do, I shall run away. . . . Think of the dust it will make when it's put in. . . . It only shows you don't think I clean the lamps properly,' she gulped out between her sobs, 'but I never expect gratitude.'

Sometimes now, when she felt particularly unhappy, she would run out into the churchyard that adjoined the house and throw herself at full length on her mother's grave. For this display she would seem to prefer to choose a rainy night, and would lie prone there, sobbing her heart out, until her wet and weary father, who had observed her leave the house, and had soon come to know the ritual, would arrive to drag her off the stone and take her home. She would allow herself to be led, but, on reaching the house, would at once, without waiting to change her sodden clothes, run downstairs and begin to rake out the kitchen stove, and spin round among the ashes, until her dress, clinging to her form, would assume the look of a plaster cast, and her pretty face, its delicate skin still wet from mingled tears and rain, would be caked, as if with a mud mask at a beauty specialist's.

One night at dinner a piteous scene arose when, as Cinderella offered her father a dish, he glanced at her dress and observed kindly :

'''Rella, child, I was thinking you should come out of mourning now. Your dear mother has been dead for over a year, and it isn't suitable for you at your age to go about for the rest of your life in black. So I've ordered you three new dresses from Paris — you're seventeen now and should begin to take an interest in your clothes.'

At these words, Cinderella fled from the room in a passion of tears, and for the rest of the night Wilfer Old Hall was loud with her sobs. . . . When the dresses came, she would not wear them, for though she often complained of how busy she was, she liked to make her own clothes, and to darn and mend her father's shirts. Her mother had also taught her how to wash her father's socks : and this she always did herself, shrinking them to the quick, so that they became an agony to him — but he had to put them on, or she would cry. And after a good day's washing and shrinking, it was noticeable how much the child would enjoy her tea and toast.

In spite of the companionship that Cinderella offered him, it seems that her father after a time began to feel somewhat lonely, and proposed marriage to a neighbour and old friend. Lily Lady Laughingtower was a good-natured, plump, concentric widow, built on the model, as it were, of an old-fashioned cottage loaf, only with a head stuck on at the top : but her dress still carried on the tradition of the years when she had been a handsome, rather florid young woman. She liked to dwell much on that period — to which invariably she referred as 'the old days'. Though garrulous, she was vague at the same time, so that she never could properly remember any single one of the many incidents she set out to

describe, and hunted the truth down its tortuous burrows
for many an hour. She possessed, Cinderella's father
was aware, a kindly disposition, and could be trusted to
be considerate to his daughter. He had felt too, it may
be, that his new wife's two grown-up girls — they were
just three and two years older respectively than Cinderella,
— would be company for her. But Cinderella herself
did not share this opinion, and on learning the news
of his engagement, and for many days thereafter, had
refused all sustenance and cried incessantly.

It is not my business to tell you of the wedding —
that is another story for another day — but I must record
that while at first Cinderella had feared that her feelings
would not allow her to attend the ceremony, which was
to take place in the capital, yet in the end she had recognised that it was her duty to master them, and was
accordingly present, albeit she still wore mourning. With
the light, bouquet-like dresses of the other relations and
guests, this made a striking contrast : and, indeed, she
was very noticeable, for she had become — it was remarked almost for the first time — unusually pretty,
with her ash-blond hair showing its pale gold from under
a black bonnet, and with her complexion, which was at
the same time pale and brilliant, with that pallor of the
very fair, enabling her mother's old friends who were
present to say not only that she was 'lovely', but also
that she looked 'pinched and white' and 'sweet and re-
signed to everything'. They proceeded to wonder in a
whisper that resounded, whether her father gave her

enough to eat, or was starving her as he had starved her mother : 'Poor old Lily ! she little knows. Her weight will soon reduce itself without any trouble to her. At any rate, she'll be saved the expense of slimming pills,' they added spitefully.

All through the service, Cinderella indulged in a quiet soprano sob, and afterwards, at the wedding-breakfast, which was in a hotel, she still maintained, at any rate in public, her fast. But she showed some sign of affection for Lady Laughingtower, who had always been very kind to her. Before the marriage, Cinderella had given her no present, but now, when for a moment there was a silence, in front of everyone she rushed demonstratively at her stepmother, kissed her, and drawing from the black bosom of her own dress an object, thrust it into the bride's hand, saying simply through her tears :

'I feel I must give you something — and this is all I have to give.'

The guests crowded round to see the present, which proved to be an oval miniature of Cinderella's mother in a plain gilt frame.

For an instant the recipient had seemed rather taken aback, but before she could say anything, Cinderella had jumped up and kissed her again, and then had darted away. 'How charming of her !' most people cried. 'What a *sweet* thought !' . . . With a final sob, Cinderella proceeded to run out of the hotel, and refusing several offers of lifts in various motor-cars belonging to her friends, hurried home. Tired and footsore though

cousin, so belittlingly known as *Common Cold* : (*Common*,
indeed, with so much resource and vitality, and yet so
dignified in its old-fashioned manifestations !). There,
again, passed *Typhoid minimus* known as *Para B*. This
teeming world, moreover, included many strange and
rare organisms, of unidentifiable visage, beaked or saucer-
faced, and of a potentiality not yet to be gauged, though
they were undoubtedly already on the look-out for
the right victim. As they passed, they would regard
Cinderella's father — or so it seemed to him — with a
frank air of unappeased hunger : and as he saw this,
and slunk away, it would occur to him how strange it
was that, though it was often true that he who took up
the sword perished by the sword, yet she who stirred
up the much more lethal dust appeared always to be
totally impervious to its effect. His first wife had never
ailed until her death, nor did Cinderella ever pass a day
in bed. But perhaps the kindly manner in which they
fed the hungry and turbulent armies with horrible-
smelling disinfectants (on which they seemed to thrive
as heartily as clothes-moths are obviously invigorated by
naphtha, camphor and all these delicious and delicate
varieties of moth-balls), or gave them tea-leaves, spread
for a while to lie over them like a brown, warm, wet
blanket, which not only helped to nourish and keep fit
the adult germ, but also, more important, helped to
hatch and incubate the spawn — perhaps these acts of
grace assured Cinderella, and had assured her mother
before her, of a special place in microbic affection. . . .

So it was with real terror that Cinderella's father perceived the yellow, quarantine banners of the dust hanging
out from every window to welcome him and his bride.
Further, today was Boiler Day and the day appointed
for cleaning the kitchen flues, and as they entered the
hall, the victorious columns could be seen enclosing the
whole staircase. The texture, he noticed, was a little
different, lacked all glitter, darkened the air, even outside the house, with a particular fat thickness and opacity,
like that of a fog, while Cinderella's face, when at last
they found her revolving furiously at the storm's very
centre, had every line, at other times invisible, incised,
apparently engrained with green and black dust, until it
resembled the mask of a Tibetan devil-dancer. . . . But
her stepmother seemed pleased with the display.

'You seldom find a gal like that nowadays,' she
observed to her husband, 'very seldom. I take my hat
off to her. Pamela and Diana are too busy enjoying
themselves to worry about housework. But there — as
dear old Laughingtower used to say in the old days —
"One can only be young once". . . . I remember how
angry he was when at the end of a story he'd told twice
running, dear old boy, he said it, and Huntminster, one
of his friends, said rudely, "Yes, you can only be young
once, but you can be childish twice". — And that reminds me, Victor, I thought it touching of your gal
to give me that present.' . . . But though Lily Lady
Laughingtower — as she still elected to be called after
her second marriage — was not aware of it, Cinderella

F

had just made her, through the agency of the dust, as she talked, a second and more considerable gift : a sore throat which imposed on the bride ten days in bed, and a further week given over to recuperation.

In the course of time, though, she recovered, and life at Wilfer Old Hall began to fall into a familiar pattern. Lily Lady Laughingtower, though her illness had at first made her irritable, tried to be kind — but even she found it did not always prove easy, because Cinderella only lived for her work. To wean her from it a little, her stepmother succeeded in engaging, after several weeks of search, a Latvian fishwife to serve in the dining-room, and a displaced Jewess from Haifa to act as house-maid : but though they had been so hard to find, they could not be persuaded to stay more than one month, because Cinderella so often chid them and interfered with their work. A superannuated so-called 'music-hall artiste' from Cernauti, and a green-faced Egyptian house-boy replaced them : but it was at this moment that Cinderella chose to introduce the Rite of Spring Cleaning — the equivalent of those ceremonies with which the Arctic and Tartar tribes welcome the Spring Solstice — twice a year instead of once, and they quitted also. But this made it no better or worse. If poor Lady Laughing-tower went out for a minute, she would return to find that Cinderella had 'done out' her room. The dust had been shifted into new corners, and each piece of furniture had been moved somewhere else than where it should be, every book, every hairbrush had been hidden. Nor did these poltergeist-like manifestations by any means exhaust the child's resource and energy. In the absence of her stepmother and sisters on some shopping expedition, for example, she would mend and darn their clothes, so that no single one of them could appear again in public for several days without discomfort. It seemed there was *nothing* that Cinderella would not do for them. She even cleaned her stepmother's shoes. She used to rake out the grates, lay the fires — though she did not believe in warm rooms : it wasn't healthy —, polish the floors (till walking became a sport, like skating, only involuntary, and Lily Lady Laughingtower and her two large, easy-going daughters would find themselves ricochetting across the room faster than any expert skier could race down a mountain slope), and make the beds with such rigour that it was impossible to untuck the bedclothes without incurring a semi-dislocation of the wrist. . . . Only on Sundays would she take an hour off to go to Early Service in Wilfer Church. Then, at an hour which shamed the rest of the household, she could be heard marching through the house with a very loud, ostentatiously uncomplaining tread and creak. Sometimes, too, if in particularly bad humour, she would sing, as she ran downstairs — the scale, it might be, trilled out like a lark, but a sudden shriek would cut it short as she would catch her foot and fall. For a week following such an accident, she would wear a bandage round her ankle, and though she still continued to perform every one of her self-appointed tasks, her smile

Gallet Parma-Violet. . . . I was going to leave off work for half an hour, but now I see I'm grudged even that amount of leisure !'

For the rest of the day Cinderella remained locked in her room, sobbing and moaning like a harmonium. . . . Diana and Pamela were obliged to acknowledge to each other that life seemed nevertheless a little easier for them when she chose thus to immure herself. There were not so many booby-traps and, even with the continual howling, the house seemed quieter.

'All the same,' Diana confessed to Pamela, 'it makes one feel such a beast to say so. Think of everything she does for us ! I know she'd go through fire and water.'

Lily Lady Laughingtower also paid her tribute : ''Mazin' what that gal does ! In the old days at Laughingtower, it would have taken ten housemaids to raise that same amount of dust. But that's what I've always said. "Do it ourselves and SHOW THEM !" . . . Not an easy gal, mind you. As Laughingtower said one night to King Dodon at dinner, when he refused champagne, "You can lead a horse to the trough, but you can't make him drink". King Dodon looked very angry and . . .' — but just then her story was cut short by a crash outside.

After any little difference of opinion, Lady Laughingtower and her daughters would soon be reconciled to Cinderella, and in token of it would frequently buy her little gifts, new clothes and shoes : but she would put them away at once and never wear them, saying, 'They're not suitable for my work'. Thus when she came into the drawing-room, as very occasionally she did, to see old friends of her mother who had happened to call, they would be startled at the contrast presented by Cinderella's faded cotton dress, broken-down shoes and dusty, disarranged hair, with the rich, decorative, clean appearance of her stepmother and stepsisters.

'Poor child, poor Cinderella, to be so neglected!' the visitors would exclaim subsequently to their neighbours. 'I never saw such neglect. That wicked old Lady Laughingtower and her two daughters ought to be ashamed of themselves! But it's always the way with a second marriage.'

Pamela and Diana were in truth by no means greedy, yet sometimes they were made to feel so. All young girls — and old girls too — love jewels, and one day when Cinderella's father was just setting off for an expedition to the capital, he assembled the family together, and said:

'Darlings, I have an announcement to make. . . . I have just won thirty thousand pounds in a football-pool, and would like to buy each of you a present. . . . Lily, you choose first.'

Lady Laughingtower asked for a piece of jewellery she had seen in a shop recently, a fox-terrier in diamonds, with its head on one side, with eyes of ruby, and wearing a beret of pale sapphires. (It would be a useful ornament, she said, as it could be worn either as a brooch or a pendant.) Pamela chose a necklace of small pearls, and Diana,

emeralds, but Cinderella, with a smile of noticeable sweetness, said :

'Daddy, darling, all I want is the first twig that
knocks against your hat on the way home. Break it
off for me.'

So that evening he returned with a diamond terrier
for Lily Lady Laughingtower, a pearl necklace and clasp
from Cartier for Pamela, and an emerald clip from Van
Cleef for Diana. As he approached home, he wondered
what he could find for Cinderella, because naturally he
had not knocked against any tree, and was not likely to,
for he was a tidy man who looked where he was going —
but just at that moment, as he was passing the gardener's
shed, it so happened that in fact he did collide in the
darkness with a besom sticking out of the darkness from
a shelf, and a piece of it broke against his hat. Accordingly he picked up the twig and, without feeling it
necessary to explain its origin, presented it to Cinderella
when he gave the jewels to the other members of the
family. . . . Cinderella thanked him and kissed him,
then slipped out of the house to visit her mother's grave,
and on it planted the twig, which she watered with her
tears. This she continued to do every day until it had
grown into a beautiful little tree.

It was about now, when she was approaching the age
of eighteen, that she began to have singular experiences.
. . . One night she was in her room, combing her pale
mermaid's locks in front of a looking-glass, when she
heard a fluttering — if it were not a contradiction, one

would say a ponderous fluttering — and turning round, she saw a lady with fair hair, in which shone a diamond star. She wore white wings and a white ball-dress covered with silver sequins, rather old-fashioned in style. The expression on her face was somewhat vacuous, but happy. The lady spoke in a voice of sugar and silver, at once tremulous but convinced of virtue.

'Cinderella !' she said, 'you have two godmothers. I am the good fairy : (of the other, I prefer to say nothing). I, and I alone, can help you. Poor child ! You are a victim of self-pity. You need taking out of yourself. You stay too much in the house. Above all, you fear fresh air. This is because,' she added somewhat pro-saically and with a doctrinaire manner, 'you suffer from an Oedipus-complex. You only feel safe behind the wall of dust and cinders you create. In other words, and put more plainly, you are, without being aware of it, in love with your father. But psycho-analysis can come to your aid. . . . Let me put to you some helpful questions. Look !' — and here she suddenly produced a diamond wand — 'look at this wand of mine and tell me what it makes you think of. . . . Be honest with yourself, child !' . . . But at this moment Cinderella woke up, as she came later to conclude, or else the fairy vanished.

When the first season of Spring Cleaning was at its height, the King decided that his only son should give two entertainments at the Palace. Excitement among those who had been invited — and equally among those who had not — mounted higher every day : though I find the reason for this rather hard to explain to the English reader, who has not undergone similar experiences. I must, however, make some attempt at elucidation. . . . The country, then, in which Cinderella lived was called Grudgeland, an island which was at the head of a mighty empire, and differed greatly from our country in customs and epoch. The inhabitants of this strange and far land had always been famous for their love of freedom and for their common sense. Recently they had been engaged in two victorious wars. The first had been a straightforward, line-up, challenge-cup fight : but the second we must examine more carefully, because the way in which it was not only led up to, but conducted, provided a triumphant vindication of the principles and wisdom of the Government, and of the people who put it in power, and demonstrated once and for all the superiority of democratic statesmanship over all other systems. . . . The second war started ostensibly — though other causes may have entered in — because Grudgeland, traditionally opposed to tyranny of every sort, had guaranteed the independence of Krakovia — a gesture, it was generally recognised, all the more noble because Grudgeland lacked at that moment any means of implementing its guarantee. Krakovia, a land without a natural seaport, the only one in such a situation in the whole of the Continent, was also the only one of which Grudgeland, a sea power, had guaranteed the frontiers : moreover it was squeezed between two hostile, greedy and tyrannical powers :

Tartary, ruled by the Red Boyar, and Hunland by the White Despot. The guarantee given by Grudgeland encouraged Krakovia to resist all demands made on it, and accordingly the White Despot ordered his army, the most formidable in numbers and the most ingeniously mechanised in the world, to attack her. Automatically, therefore, Cinderella's motherland had become involved in war : though since she lacked all arms, she could do nothing for several months except boast of what she was going to do when she got them, and make the most intimidating series of faces at the enemy. (One of her statesmen excelled at this.) When at last prepared, however, her people fought, as always, like lions, for they were by nature courageous and persistent, and put themselves to untold exertions, and decreed for themselves the most severe deprivations — for instance, in the name and cause of freedom, the suppression of all freedom for ten years. The White Despot's hold on Krakovia was, after a long and exhausting struggle — during the course of which Grudgeland, by insisting on supplying herself and everyone else with weapons, and on manufacturing nothing else except arms, made a present of her formerly enormous foreign trade to her chief competitors — finally weakened, and then destroyed. The power of Hunland was utterly demolished.

At this moment, Grudgeland and her allies suddenly gave away Krakovia, for whose national existence they had waged a war for seven years, to its other enemy, the Red Boyar. The world was naturally astonished at the logical principles of statesmanship this policy exemplified, and impressed by the endurance of the people of Grudgeland in support of it.   The result of the war was welcomed by great crowds in the capital of Grudgeland, singing moodily and rather out of tune the national hymn, 'Grudglings never, never, never will be drudges.' . . . But having thus victoriously attained the objects for which it went to war, Grudgeland now found that it was so poor — though wonderfully wise and heroic, as well as virtuous — that both men and women had perforce to work all day long on very reduced sustenance (this they did not mind, so long as *no one* had enough), and fortunately never had time or energy to wonder what they had fought for, or when the next war would be. . . . No, their whole object was to be ready to join in the Third War, when it should come, so as to be able to emerge a third time with laurels and hold the Challenge Cup, fashioned of uranium — for I forgot to explain that, though at first from the view of cynical foreign politicians it may seem an unexpected and almost undesirable result, yet the whole set-up had been so cleverly contrived by the Grudgling statesmen, that crawling out with triumph from the ruins at the end of the Second War, Grudgeland found she had helped to make her chief enemy, the country of the Red Boyar, the most powerful in the world, and that she now seemed nearer the outbreak of a Third, and still more appalling, War, than she had appeared to be near the Second a month before its out-break. . . . However, this discursion must not lead us too far from our story. The country, I was telling you, was so poor that there was little amusement permitted, except gambling (which every day increased), and wearing paper-hats and swinging wooden rattles at foot-ball matches. Therefore, now that the Prince was to give two parties, excitement seethed. . . . Cinderella, Pamela, Diana, were all invited — and Cinderella accepted, so that at the last moment she could refuse to go. This, however, she did not divulge to her stepsisters, who were delighted to think that she was for once to accompany them, until she was actually helping them to dress and arrange their hair. Then, when they said to her :

'Now, darling, it's your turn, we'll come and help you put your clothes on,' she looked at them reproach-fully, and said :

'You know quite well I can't go. What am I to wear ?'

Pamela and Diana were amazed at this, and said :

'Surely you remember that you've got that lovely new dress that Mama ordered specially for you from Paris. She'll be so hurt if you don't wear it.'

At these words Cinderella burst into tears, remarking :

'You seem to think that all the work in the house gets itself done. After all, *someone* has to do it.'

She then fled upstairs, her tears still falling, and bolted herself into her attic.

They tried their best to persuade her to change her mind. Even Lily Lady Laughingtower climbed the stairs and endeavoured to argue with her through the door : but in the end the rest of the party was obliged to leave without her. Pamela and Diana felt uneasy, almost unhappy, thinking of poor Cinderella at home, dusting : but when at last they entered the ballroom, looked round on the scene, and saw the Prince, these thoughts left them.

As her stepmother's kind, rich voice floated up to Cinderella at the window, saying, 'Goodbye, 'Rella ! Take care of yourself !', and as she heard the motor start and drive away, she began almost to wish that she had gone to the ball too. . . . But, she asked herself, how could she have done so ? The truth of the matter was, they always left her behind : she was just a drudge — and here she afforded herself the indulgence of a good cry. . . . Soon, however, she tired of this particular expression of her grief — after all, she was young —, so she unlocked the door and, after creeping through the empty house, where everything seemed tonight unnaturally quiet, let herself out at the back entrance, and ran to visit her mother's grave. This time, she did not throw herself on it, for her father had gone to the ball too, and so there was no one to fetch her in — besides, it was a fine night. . . . She looked at the grave and, hardly knowing what she did, broke off a small branch of the birch tree that had grown from the besom-twig, and waved it in the air. As she did so, some strange, strong impulse seized on her to repeat quickly a few nonsensical words that had strung themselves together in her head, and came unbidden to her lips :

> '*Horse and Hattock,*
> *Horse and go,*
> *Horse and Pelatis,*
> *Ho, ho !* '

It sounded almost like a spell, she reflected — but at that moment her thoughts were distracted, for she felt a sudden wave of ice-cold air, and then there was a whir-ring, coming nearer all the while, like the approach of a V.1 bomb, until out of the darkness spoke a voice of rather harsh tone :

'I can't leave my coven for long just now, until the ceremonies are over : but I'll come round later.'

Cinderella could not think what the words meant — she must have been dreaming again : but she soon forgot all about it and went home.

Since the rest of the family was out, she decided to stand herself a really good meal as a treat, and began at once to prepare it. So fully occupied was she by this task that only very occasionally, as she thought, for example, of her stepsisters arriving at the Palace, or later, pictured them entering the ballroom, did she cry. But it was during one of these moments of weakness that she heard, immediately behind her, the same voice that had spoken in the graveyard.

'What is the matter, my poor child ?' it asked. Cinderella hastily let drop upon the stone floor the Meissen china basket in which she had been arranging some fresh figs and nectarines for her supper, and looked round. . . . There, quite near her, stood a striking-looking old lady, with what people who did not take to her at first sight might have called a hump-back. Her nose was prominent and decided, and the end of it nearly touched her chin, on which, Cinderella noticed, grew — well, not a beard exactly, but a slight down. Her hair was cut short, she wore no hat, and she was dressed in a smartly tailored black coat and skirt, without ornament except for a diamond and platinum clip on the lapel ; a piece of good unobtrusive jewellery, which Cinderella examined more closely — and found to represent a broomstick. In her hand the old lady carried an ebony cane. . . . Cinderella regarded her for some moments without saying anything, and thought to herself ; 'What a nice expression she has ! You can see she has suffered. I should love to hear her story' ; but then, looking down, and seeing the pieces of her father's favourite china basket on the kitchen pavers, she set herself to cry with renewed application and vigour.

The old lady, following the direction of Cinderella's eyes, exclaimed, 'Is that all that's the matter ? Watch me ! See what I can do !' and waved her stick above the fragments. The wonder-struck girl saw them thereupon begin to wriggle and jump centripetally upon the floor, until they had joined themselves together and the dish was whole again. . . . There was an instant of silence, then the old lady resumed :

'Did no one ever tell you that you had a fairy-god-mother, Cinderella ?'

'Well, certainly the other night a lady in white chiffon, and with a diamond star in her hair, came to see me and said something about——'

'I know her, the simpering, silly bit,' the old lady interrupted angrily, 'for ever "trying to help", and believing that all evil has a rational basis and can be purged from the mind — but don't let us even talk of her.   She's not worth it. . . . Has no one else ever told you ?'

'I believe my mother' — and here, at the loved name, Cinderella burst into tears again (from surprise when the Meissen dish had been re-created, she had stopped crying) — 'once mentioned to me, madam, that I had a god-mother — or was it two godmothers ?' (she saw the old lady frown at this), 'but I thought she had forgotten me.'

'That's right, dear,' the stranger said, patting Cinder-ella kindly on the shoulder, 'always have your cry out — though sometimes you may find it more effective,' she added, 'to restrain your tears, so long as you allow the effort it costs you to be clearly seen.'

'Now that *is* good of you,' Cinderella said, grateful for the technical hint.   'I hadn't thought of that !'

'*I* never forget my godchildren,' the old lady con-tinued, 'and I watch their development, and come to help them when they need it. . . . Tell me, child, wouldn't you like to go to the Prince's Ball ?   I could still arrange it for you.   You would enjoy yourself there, and your sisters need never know, for you would be back here before them.'

'But how can I go? I've got no clothes, only an old dress my stepmother gave me,' Cinderella said, not quite truthfully, 'and she and the two girls would recognise it. Besides, the Palace is a long way off. I can't possibly walk there, and I've no money to hire a car — even if there were time now to find one.'

'I like your approach to things. I can see you don't take life too easily, and know how to repine effectively. But never mind for once, dear. If you wish to go, do as I tell you. . . . Run into the kitchen-garden, and fetch me the largest pumpkin you can find.'

Much puzzled, Cinderella obeyed. . . . In a few moments she returned, carrying an enormous, rugged, golden, globe-like fruit of that cucurbitaceous plant.

The old lady took it from her, put it on the kitchen-table, and cut it open in a business-like way — as if she was used to the process — with a long knife — but there, in the middle, instead of seeds, were several microfilm documents headed *Most Secret*.

'Bother!' said the old lady. 'Of course, it's the confidential papers from the State Department. I'd forgotten in which pumpkin my agents had hidden them. It's rather awkward! But never mind, we've other things to think of!' . . . And hastily wiping the microfilms with a napkin, she put them in the pocket of her coat, and continued to clean out the centre of the fruit. After a while, she looked up from her task and added :

G

'Now go to the pantry, and see if there are any mice in the trap.'

'There are sure to be,' Cinderella replied, 'because Pamela and Diana are both always so wasteful, leaving bits of food about. Couldn't you teach them, madam, to be more tidy ? It would serve them right to be given a good lesson !'

'You're quite my favourite god-child, Cinderella. You have a lot of your dear mother in you : you speak just like her — and I was much attached to her. . . . You, too, will be a real help to any man you marry ; I can see that — but we mustn't stop here talking all night ! Go and find the mice.'

Cinderella came back shortly, with a trap containing one large mouse and six small ones.

The old lady thanked her, and added :

'Go once more to the kitchen-garden, and look in the crevices of the wall behind which you found the pumpkin, and you'll see some lizards. Catch them and bring them to me.'

Once more Cinderella complied.

'Now,' said her godmother, 'shut your poor red eyes while I count seven.'

Cinderella did as she was told, for she found it easy to obey the fascinating old lady : but she did not stop up her ears, and could distinguish the tapping of the large ebony cane, and the sound of hurrying footsteps, as well as the clump of hooves.

'. . . Six. . . . Seven ! Open your eyes, child !'

Through the kitchen window, Cinderella saw a magnificent gold coach drawn by six plump and rosy horses of the extinct Hanoverian breed, with long, creamy tails and manes. Behind the coach, and attached to it, in the style of its period, were two allegorical figures also carved and gilded, and representing Virtue overcoming Vice — or Vice overcoming Virtue, Cinderella could not be sure which. A fat coachman in a wig and state livery sat on the box, and six footmen were in attendance, wearing black silk knee-breeches, white silk stockings and coats of sepia velvet, with waistcoats frogged with gold. Cinderella noticed that on their gold buttons they carried as crest a broomstick rampant.

'Well, get in, dear, or you'll be late,' the old lady commanded.

Cinderella was just about to leave the house, thinking to herself, 'I won't change my dress. I'll go just as I am and shame them,' when at that very moment the old lady touched her on the shoulder with her ebony cane, and to Cinderella's amazement and consternation, her torn and discoloured cotton dress became cloth-of-silver, and her bare legs were covered in the finest nylon stockings. She began to cry again, — until she saw her shoes, which so surprised her that she stopped : for her small feet were now cased in slippers made of glass — rather *outré*, Cinderella considered, but pretty, all the same.

'Hurry, my dear,' the old lady urged her, 'your new clothes are all part of my plan, so don't let them upset you. And I must tell you, so that you can be prepared, that at the last stroke of midnight, if you have not already left the Palace, your coach will become a pumpkin again, your servants and horses will turn to mice and lizards, and your cloth-of-silver dress will become patched cotton once more.'

On hearing this, Cinderella brightened. She might make something of it. 'And, after all,' she reflected, 'the old lady seems to know her own game. So I must put my trust in her judgement, and make the best of it !'

As the coach drove up the processional route to the Palace, its obsolete but glittering splendours caused a stir among the chauffeurs of the grand motor-cars, brought out for the occasion — usually it was impossible to obtain petrol —, and lined up and waiting. The crowd at the gates first gaped and then cheered. 'It must be the Lord Mayor's daughter,' one or two cried.

The Prince was dancing with Pamela as Cinderella entered the ballroom, but the music stopped suddenly and all the dancers were arrested in their movements, as if every flutter of every leaf in the world were all at once to be stilled. This cessation had about it a singular beauty, the reverse — but much more rare — of that which is to be observed when a dance begins, and the whole planetary system starts to break, rustle and sway. . . . As she advanced, Cinderella had noticed among the faces of those she passed, who stood as if entranced, several that were familiar to her from the pages of the newspapers. (For instance, near her, by the buffet directly outside the door, impressively alone in his rough working clothes among all the jewelled ladies and the men in court dress, stood the ascetic figure of the great democratic orator, Mr. Laski Bollinger, the new Minister of National Penury — it must be explained that he came thus garbed in order to call less attention to himself.) As the newcomer walked on, into the centre of the room, a dazzling, perturbing figure, slight, with her ash-fair hair this time un-dusted by cinders and with her radiant skin un-lined, and un-incised with soot, and offering, indeed, a peach-like texture lacking in many of the beautiful faces round her, a sigh broke the silence, as if someone were stirring to life again, and the Prince walked slowly across the floor to meet her. . . . The very first moment he had caught sight of the stranger, he had dropped the hand of his partner, Pamela, for he had thought — as had many of those present — that this must be the unknown Princess, who, it had been rumoured, would make her appearance that evening.

So sparkling and unresigned did Cinderella look that night, her complexion diamantine at the touch of her god-mother's wand, that her stepsisters did not recognise her, though, as they stood together by the wall and watched, Diana remarked to Pamela :

'Odd ! Don't you think that the lovely girl who has just come in has a look of Cinderella ? It only shows what she could make of herself if she would take a little trouble with her appearance. . . . I still feel such a beast for having left her at home, — but what could one do ?'

Pamela, carefully examining the newcomer, agreed with Diana. Indeed the two sisters, handsome and large, were not even annoyed with the stranger who put them in the shade for the whole evening : since the Prince, with whom each had fallen in love at first sight, and who had hitherto paid them great attention, dancing with one or the other the whole time until Cinderella had arrived, now never came near them. No one, moreover, approached them, either to talk or to ask for a dance. But no element of spite or envy existed in their natures.

For Cinderella the hours flew by all too swiftly, yet at the same time they seemed to absorb a whole summer, so that at moments she was sure midnight would never strike. The King's son had led her in to supper at the head of a procession of dignitaries, and for once all desire to snub or retreat into herself had left her, and in a mood new to her, of contentment or even of happiness, she was lost to time. . . . Suddenly looking up at the clock in the Banqueting Hall, she saw it was ten minutes to twelve, and rising from the table hurriedly, and rather unceremoniously, she cried, 'I must leave, I must go at once !' The Prince expostulated, but seeing that she had made up her mind, accompanied her to the door. . . . Perhaps in a way the manner of her departure only served to deepen the sense of mystery that had surrounded her from the moment she arrived. So exquisite in her fragile fashion did she look as she went out, that many

of the guests forgot their manners, and stood on their
seats to see her go by and waved their handkerchiefs at
her. . . . And Cinderella, as the Prince handed her into
her coach and she drove off, without any semblance of
looking to left or right, obtained, for her part, a very
satisfactory glimpse of Pamela and Diana standing together near a wall, and without having any man in
attendance on either, or even both, of them.

Once inside, the motion of the lumbering vehicle
made her quickly fall asleep ; a long, restless stretch of
slumber, during which the lady in white chiffon had
again materialised. First, Cinderella had seen a star
through the open window, and then it had turned to a
diamond star in the hair of the lady, who came floating
in at the aperture, steadying herself, as she entered, by
holding on to the door-handle, so that Cinderella quite
feared the stranger might fall out and kill herself.
Directly she had found her sea-legs — for she would not
sit down —, she began to address Cinderella with uneasy
dignity :

'Poor, poor child ! You think you have enjoyed
yourself ! But I am your *good* godmother, and know all
that has happened. Beware of the old woman in black.
She seeks your worldly advancement : whereas I seek
only your good. . . . Little did I think to live to see a
god-daughter of mine drive in a mouse-coach, attended
by lizards ! Child ! believe me, it is all due to your
Inferiority Complex. You must rid yourself of it. *I*
can promise you no brilliant marriages, but a clean, sane,

healthy life of hard work, and a pension at sixty. But you must first promise to give up seeing your wicked godmother. Then, I will guarantee you a good course of psycho-analysis. I might arrange for you to be sent to one of the Bloomsbury schools — I'd pay for it myself — and later I'll try to persuade Professor Zinckmeiss of Vienna to lift from you your Oedipus burden.' . . . With these words, she flew out again, fluttering out of the window like a white silk curtain caught in the wind.

Cinderella woke up before she reached home. She alighted from the coach, turned the door-handle and walked in. But no sooner had her glass slippers crossed the threshold than, once more, she was in her bare feet and old cotton gown. She ran straight to the kitchen, and there she found her real godmother waiting for her. Directly the dear old lady saw Cinderella, she opened the window, leant out, tapped the coach with her stick, and then bent down, and picked up from the ground outside the shell of a large golden pumpkin cut in half, that lay just where the coach had been a moment before. Hastily taking some microfilms out of her pocket, she thrust them into the centre of the fruit, put on top the other half, which lay on the table, touched the reconstituted pumpkin with her cane, and there it was, whole again ! . . . Then, turning to Cinderella, she said approvingly :

'Obedient child ! I hope you enjoyed yourself. . . . There will be another ball at the Palace tomorrow night — as I do not need, I can see from your face, to remind you. You can be present at it on the same terms as to-

night, and with the same equipage : but bear in mind
that if you have not taken your departure by the time the
clock strikes midnight — well, you're left there, just as
you stand now, in your old dress and bare feet.'

Cinderella, after experiencing an evening of personal
triumph, of which she could not but be aware, found
herself rather piqued by such conditions being repeated :
fairy godmother or no fairy godmother, she had now no
intention of allowing herself to be patronised, so she
answered :

'Between ourselves, madam, I have some very pretty
dresses put away upstairs, that my stepmother gave me
and that I have never worn. . . . I could go to the ball
in one of them, and then I should not have to leave at
twelve.'

'I know quite well all about your dresses without
your having to tell me, thank you, Cinderella. But may
I bring to your attention the fact that, before you went
out, you told me you had no new dresses ? Whatever
happens to you, you should learn not to contradict yourself !' the old lady replied rather sharply. Then, soften-
ing a little, she added, 'But where is your common
sense, child ? Your suggestion would not fall in with
our plans. We have to pretend that your family allow
you no clothes, and won't let you go to any parties.'

With those words, she vanished, whirring away into
the distance. . . . A moment later a motor-car drove up,
and out of it, looking very tired and rather dispirited,
stepped the rest of the family. Lily Lady Laughing-

tower was, however, still talking in animated fashion, telling her husband of the ball at Rumscuttle — her husband's place in North Grudgeland — which she had given for King Dodon IX in the old days. The girls got out of the motor and went straight up to their rooms, and Cinderella, climbing the back stairs, followed them.

'You haven't really been waiting up for us all this time, Cinderella !' they cried as she entered. 'You *oughtn't* to have done it ! You make us feel such brutes, and you must be dead tired. Go to bed at once !'

Cinderella replied, 'I didn't expect you so early. I thought, if you were really enjoying yourselves, that you wouldn't be back home before five — and it's only ten to two. I didn't at all mind stopping up. It gave me the chance to do all sorts of odd jobs that I'd not had time to start on before — such as darning and mending : you two are heavy on your clothes, you're big, one must remember. . . . Now let me help you off with your dress, Diana, or you'll tear it, as you did last time you went to a party — and I had to mend it for you. . . . But did you enjoy yourselves tonight at the ball ? And did you both dance with the Prince ? Tell me all about it while I help you off with your things.'

When they had been out of the house for a few hours, the two sisters would forget how habitually difficult Cinderella was, and how easily she took offence, and they would, until the first inevitable outbreak, treat her as an ordinary person : so now in order to amuse her they began to tell her, as she had requested them to do, of the

ball, and especially of the Princess, as people had thought
her, who had arrived, it was said, in a coach drawn by
six horses, and who had caused such a sensation in the
ballroom.   Pamela ended her description by saying :

'. . . She was wearing a wonderful silver dress, and
do you know, 'Rella, dearest, she had such a look of you.
We both noticed it.'

The next moment, however, Pamela wished she had
not spoken, because Cinderella at once started to
cry. . . . At first, she would not answer the sisters at
all, but in the end she managed to sob out :

'You are making fun of me, both of you.   You tell
me all about the ball only in order to make me feel
unhappy ! — How could I go without a dress fit to wear ?'

By this time her stepsisters were feeling very depressed
and exhausted — it really was growing late, but they
were obliged to prepare a glass of hot milk with some
rum in it for Cinderella, and to put her to bed with a
hot-water bottle.   All this business occupied some time,
and they grew more tired.   Still she would not speak to
them. . . . It was nearly four-thirty when finally they
got to their rooms — but only two and a half hours
later, at seven, they were woken by the sound of Cinderella dusting outside their rooms . . . She never seemed
to weary or to need sleep.

In the evening Cinderella again helped her sisters to
dress.   Once more they urged, even implored, her to
change her mind and come with them to the ball.

'Do come, 'Rella,' Diana entreated, 'we need support. Both Pamela and I are hopelessly in love with the Prince, and at first we thought *he* rather liked *us* : but in the end he treated us cruelly. And if the Princess comes to the ball again tonight, no doubt the same thing will happen. We really *need* someone with us, and we can't tell Mama. Do come. Say you'll come !' But she would not give in.

Thus they stayed arguing with her until the very last moment, when Lily Lady Laughingtower and Cinderella's father were already in the motor and began impatiently calling the girls to join them. Hurriedly they got in at last, but not before they had been given time to see that Cinderella was now again in tears at being left behind.

Alone in Wilfer, Cinderella began to think of her poor mother and to feel more than ever mournful and deserted by the world, when, from the opposite direction the motor had taken, came a sound of wheels and of hooves, and there was her coach again, with the same footmen in attendance. . . . She was just beginning to wonder what had happened to her godmother, when an escort of six bats flew in at the window ; then sounded a now familiar whirring, and there was the dear old lady beside her !

'Good evening, child : your coach is waiting,' she announced and touched with her stick of ebony Cinderella's dress. This time it turned to cloth of gold, instead of silver, but the slippers were the same, of glass.

'Jump in ! There's no time to be lost. Don't wait

great advantage that Grudgeland had acquired over its neighbours as the result of the heroism and endurance its people had shown in two wars, and of the victories that had finally crowned their efforts, was that though motor-cars and aircraft were in daily use in every other country, no one in Grudgeland could afford to use them, and there was no petrol to be obtained : similarly no one could afford to buy the goods, turned out more cheaply and in greater profusion than ever before, and there was no coal for heating or lighting in the cold, dark Grudgling winters, and no new clothes for the workers, who were yet better paid — as was often pointed out to them by the Government — than ever before in the history of Grudgeland. So it was, throughout the whole range of human ingenuity, skill and endeavour. All this gave the Grudglings a moral and mental superiority of which they were immensely proud, and that none could gainsay. Foreign countries naturally envied them greatly. But the Grudglings, who were a proud race, were not going to let foreign countries confine their efforts to envy : no, they roundly demanded loans, pointing out to the rich nations from whom they demanded them that, but for Grudgling policy and efforts, there might have been no wars for foreign nations to have become involved in. Moreover, not only, in these circumstances, did they borrow money, they also lent it. . . . However, I must not stray too far, but must content myself by pointing out that it was typical of the fine simplicity of life in Grudgeland, and of the struggle made by all

classes, that though the capital possessed the finest lighting
system in the world, recently installed at great expense,
this could hardly ever, except by special decree of the
Minister of National Penury, be made use of, and then
only until midnight. . . . There was, Cinderella thought,
as she saw the lamps begin to go out, something up-
lifting about it. What other country, she reflected —
for she was most patriotic —, what other country could
equal this, with its perpetual sacrifices, culminating in
a perpetual appeal for further ones ! Any other land
would impeach those responsible for the lines of policy
that had led to this result. But not the Grudglings :
they would merely stand in a queue and demand more
punishment. . . . But she must not stand here thinking
of these things. She must go ! She must run ! And
at the second chime from the belfry of the Cathedral,
she clasped her head in her hands for a moment, and
uttered a cry — a rather affected cry, if truth is to be
told, as if it had been practised many times before with
a view to its production on this occasion — and then,
lifting her train, fled from the balcony through the ballroom and down the stairs, which descended in shallow
flights broken by even spaces, over which she ran
fleetly. . . . After her went the Prince, and after him,
hard on his heels, the guests : but Cinderella maintained
her start, moving fast as the wind, so that she was in her
coach, and off, before anyone could stop her.

Back to the balcony darted the Prince to see if his
eyes could follow the golden track of her coach, lighted

with candles, passing through the now dark streets, and thus perhaps be able to perceive what direction the un-known Princess was taking, and from this deduce whence she had come. . . . It should be easy, he reflected, for coaches were so rare, only one or two existed in the whole kingdom, and he had the night before, when handing her to her coach, noted with royal eye the crest on her footmen's buttons — a broomstick. This, too, should be easy to identify. He would ask the heralds. . . . But, as the Prince searched the darkened city beneath, he could find no sign of a coach, none at all. Back he went, down to the hall again, and cross-questioned those pre-sent, but no one, guest or servant, had seen her leave. He turned despairingly towards a room through which she had passed in her flight — at least it was empty, there were no crowds to watch him —, and there, in front of him, nearly buried in the thickness of the carpet, the glitter of some object caught his eye. . . . It was one of her glass slippers, which must have fallen off in her hurry, without her noticing it. . . . Now, at last, he held a clue.

The Prince picked it up, and the next day ordered it to be placed in a casket of gold, set round with diamonds, and caused it to be announced from the Palace that the box would be awarded to any girl who could fit the shoe on her foot. By this means he hoped to make the owner eager to claim the shoe, so as to obtain the precious box, and thus he would learn her name. (When King Dodon, who had in the course of years become rather cynical, heard of what his son had done, he sent for him and said, 'You needn't have gone to all this trouble and expense ; a modern girl doesn't drop her shoe at the Palace without knowing what she's doing. In my young days, instead of putting it in a golden casket, one would have drunk champagne out of it. . . . But times change ! You'll hear of her again, all right, and very likely will one day wish you hadn't.')

After it became known to the public that the owner of the shoe would be entitled to the gold box in which it was enshrined, as well as, in all probability, to the Prince himself, the mothers of ten thousand daughters — more than had been present at the ball — rang up the Lord Chamberlain's Office. The telephone bell sounded without stopping — but the messages received were nearly always identical.

'Is that the Lord Chamberlain's Office ? . . . I am so sorry to be a bother, but I believe my silly girl left her glass shoe at the Palace last night. . . . I didn't telephone before because I *hate* giving trouble : but we can't get another anywhere — it's rather original — so could *you* make enquiries for us ?'

When, however, it transpired that the test of ownership was the ability to fit this small glass shoe, the girls themselves would telephone — for they knew their feet would be too large — and say :

'Is that the Lord Chamberlain's Office ? Mummy said I was to ring up and say, "It's all right, I've found my glass shoe, and not to worry." '

H

Still, no one was discovered whose foot could get into the shoe. . . . The Prince remained in session at the Heralds' College, trying to trace which family, royal or noble, possessed as its crest a broomstick. But this enquiry fared no better. . . . Impatient, he at last decided to send a herald all over the land, to proclaim officially that whoever could wear the shoe upon her foot should be his bride. Consequently, when the herald arrived at a town, or even a village, hundreds of women, young and old, dark and fair, ran out to try on the shoe.

It was some ten days after the ball that the herald made his appearance on the village green at Wilfer. . . . Cinderella had passed a very troubled night. The lady with the star in her hair had contrived to get into her attic again — she supposed in a dream — and had started to preach at her once more.

'Cinderella, I am your good godmother ; believe what I say, child ! . . . You dropped your shoe at the Palace — that means that you are in love with the Prince. But you are too young for marriage. Every modern girl should make her own way. I want to see you established in a career, with your insurance card stamped and in order. To achieve this, you must be equipped. A course of reliable psycho-analysis will soon overcome your weaknesses. . . . *I* don't attempt to bribe you with golden dresses or retinues of servants — who, in my opinion, are anti-social — as your wicked godmother does. But I do venture to offer you a dozen treatments and, after they are over, a post in a Government Accounts office. . . . You say you can't add up. . . . That doesn't matter today. It may even lead to promotion. But you must start at the bottom and work your own way up.'

Cinderella became cross, she didn't want — as did almost every other girl — to go into a Government office, and when the lady in white began to hector her in this way, they had quite a tussle before she woke up. . . . This morning, therefore, she felt tired.

The herald had been expected, so Lily Lady Laughingtower had asked several young people over to luncheon, and to pass the day. She had hoped it might do Pamela and Diana good, for the two girls had seemed very depressed lately — ever since the ball, in fact — and, as their mother had remarked, more like Cinderella than like their dear selves. They would mope in corners, and cry and confide in Cinderella, each of the two telling of her love for the Prince, and how callously he had behaved. . . . Today, however, with young people all round them, they were in better spirits. And Cinderella had for once consented, in spite of her fatigue, to have luncheon with them in the dining-room : though nothing that her stepsisters or Lily Lady Laughingtower could say would persuade her to wear any other clothes except those in which she worked, her stained and darned cotton dress and her cooking-boots. The members of her family, however, were so pleased that she had at last made some concession, and had agreed to become more sociable, that they did not insist.

Thus, as I was telling you, everybody was today in better spirits, and there was much laughter when, after luncheon, they heard a trumpet sound from the green, to announce the arrival of the herald. The whole party went out to greet him. . . . It was a lovely July afternoon, one of those summer afternoons when the sky takes possession of the earth. The great blue arena of the heavens was full of huge white tents, as though a tournament were to be held aloft. Underneath, on this bright, flat, green spot of earth, altogether dwarfed by the expanse of air, a few goats grazed, tethered by chains. And here the herald stood in his playing-card clothes, chequered and formal in reds and blues, and cried, 'Oyez ! Oyez ! Oyez ! Come forward !' By his side stood a man, who, to judge from his general air, was young ; but it was impossible to be sure, for his voluminous black cloak had attached to it a hood which completely hid his face.

Several girls of the party said they were too shy to try the shoe on, and among them, both Cinderella's stepsisters attempted to evade the test, saying to Cinderella, who was determined that they should enter for it :

'Listen, dearest, we're like cart-horses : our feet are far too large.'

In the end, though, Cinderella overcame their objections, and merrily led the laughter when Pamela, the first competitor, failed to get her foot into the shoe. Then came Diana's turn, with the same result, and after her the guests were equally unsuccessful. . . . Last of all,

Cinderella crept shyly forward, in her old tattered dress and clumsy boots. Ceremoniously the herald placed a chair for her, and arranged a silk cushion for her foot. . . . Somehow, she looked very pathetic at that moment — but then, she had been practising her expression before a looking-glass for hours that morning and the previous night. . . . She stretched out her foot. The shoe fitted.

At that instant, Cinderella heard a familiarly grating voice speak just behind her.

'Prince,' it said, 'I think you had better throw off your disguise and declare yourself.'

Cinderella turned round, and there was her dear old godmother : who now removed from her lapel the diamond clip she habitually wore, and herself fastened it on Cinderella's dress. . . . In the meantime, the stranger had torn off his cloak and hood, and now stood revealed as the Prince. He seized Cinderella's hand and presented to her the casket, while the crowd acclaimed them and cried '*Long Live Our Prince and Princess !*' Then, turning with an expression of marked distaste towards Pamela and Diana, the Prince said to them :

'Goodbye, ladies ! I take from you the sister you have treated so ill.'

At these words the poor sisters at first looked astonished, and then began to cry. . . . Cinderella did not bid farewell to them at all, but got into her coach, which had just drawn up. The Prince jumped in too, and the happy couple set off on the long, slow drive to the metropolis and to the Palace. As the coach lumbered along, through the aromatic golden tunnels of the summer lanes, thick with honeysuckle and with roses, Cinderella whispered coaxingly to the Prince :

'Darling, after all, I think we really ought to ask my stepsisters, and their mother, old Lily, to our wedding.'

The Prince, answering her with a kiss, said :

'Cinderella, you are not only more beautiful than any girl I have ever met, but more compassionate and forgiving.'

Little Red Ridinghood

LITTLE RED RIDINGHOOD was an only child, and lived in a cottage with her widowed mother — the reader will have noticed that nearly all the children in fairy stories live with widowed mothers or are orphans — situated in a glade of the Great Forest. This gigantic wilderness was supposed by then to be safe for children to play in, because few wild animals of any size survived, and those that lingered on were timid — though every few years a bear, a wolf or a wild boar would be seen, and shot immediately, before it had been given time to do much mischief. Since there were no companions for her of her own age in the neighbourhood, Little Red Ridinghood had been obliged to learn to play by herself, and in consequence she had come to know the region intimately ; it held no terrors for her by day, and she liked to roam in it, and grew to love its mossy confusion, the clusters and galaxies of its northern wild flowers in the spring, in the autumn the huge, misty tangles of bryony and red berries which showed like points of flame through smoke, in the winter the first snow, rounding every contour, and unmarked as yet by the script of birds' feet, and the great green solitudes, like islands, of full summer. She came to recognise, too, with pleasure the scents of the forest, the lingering foetid smell of the fox's track, the sweetness of lime blossom, that creates a whole upper world of redolence and of insect sound, as the great population of wild bees wing their way in and out, the mushroomy freshness of damp bracken, and the unmistakable fragrance of birch trees when newly felled that adorn the air with special aromatic graces. Though for her eleven years Red Ridinghood was small, she was sturdy and liked to climb to the very top of a tree — but all these pleasures were solitary, so that, when her mother called her in from the garden early one morning where she was skipping as if her life depended on it, she felt glad to be thus interrupted, since she knew it must mean an errand, and probably that she would see people in the course of it.

'I hear your grandmother is ill in bed with one of her attacks,' her mother said to her, 'and I want you to take this custard and crock of butter to her; but remember the three things I've so often told you before — not to dawdle on the way; when you get there, not to tire the old lady out with too many questions, and above all, not to offend her by making personal remarks. And another thing, don't talk to anyone you meet on the way : he might turn out to be a wolf.'

Little Red Ridinghood paid scant attention : for she was eager to be off, since her grandmother lived at the other end of the forest ; which meant that, if she was to be back before dark, the morning would be taken up in reaching there, and the afternoon in returning home.

It gave her no time even to climb trees on the way, but nevertheless it was in a good humour that she set off, for it was a red-gold day of late autumn, with little light mists haunting the spaces under the great trees, and then, as you approached, spectrally dissolving. She must have been about half-way to her destination, singing to herself, and running along, taking great jumps, when, her attention drawn to him by some sound, she turned her head, and first saw the wolf — a large animal — padding quietly, like a dog, by her side. He sniffed the air, smiled at her, and said :

'Little Red Ridinghood, don't be frightened of me ; I merely like company. I know, indeed, that some wolves have given the whole species a bad name, so you must try not to think of me as a wolf, but merely as a fellow-traveller.'

These words he spoke in a tone that was pleading and ingratiating, because, though he had not eaten a good meal for many days, he did not dare to consume his new prey yet, since he had noticed men at work in the forest, some felling trees, others collecting large pine-cones and stacking them up, and he knew they would be sure to hear the child's cries for help, and give the alarm — and that would be the end of him, appetite and all !

Red Ridinghood, who did not at first much care for the look of the so-friendly animal, took some time to answer : indeed, she danced and hopped in front of him on the path, every now and then kicking an occasional stone. In fact, on several occasions she very nearly dropped her basket which contained her mother's gifts to her grandmother. Finally, she objected with the petulant logic of children :

'It's all very well to announce yourself as a fellow-traveller, but you don't know yet where I'm going.'

'Oh yes, I do,' the wolf responded merrily. 'So far as I'm concerned, you all go the same way home.' As he thought of the meal in front of him, he spoke with an air of such infectious gaiety that it completely vanquished Red Ridinghood's doubts of him, and she now stopped fidgeting and answered the wolf in the same bantering tone he had adopted.

'But I'm not going *home*,' she said, 'I'm walking away from it, to visit my grandmother who lives in the first house by the mill in the next village.'

'How small the world is !' the wolf replied delightedly. 'That is precisely where I'm going. Gran is an old friend of mine.'

The wolf's familiarity of manner made Red Ridinghood somewhat uneasy again. She corrected him: 'No one ever calls her "Gran". We call her *Grandmother*.'

'So we do !' barked the wolf. 'I'd forgotten. The old lady trusts me, as I ask you to do, and always treats me with great kindness. . . . One day, but only when I'm really hungry, she'll make me a wonderful meal.'

'Yes, she's a splendid cook,' Red Ridinghood agreed, 'she always bakes buns and little cakes for me when she knows I'm coming to see her — but today we shan't get anything, for she is ill in bed.'

'A pity, that,' the wolf remarked. 'I was hoping to find her in prime condition — but it won't really make much difference : appetite is the main thing and—' but he broke off in what he was saying, for suddenly he detected a sound of sawing near by ; in a lower voice he added :

'I'll tell you what we'll do, we'll take different paths, and see who gets to Grandmother's first : and whichever wins must wait for the other outside the house. . . . Above all, if you're the lucky one and the old lady happens to see you arriving, don't let her know that you met me on the way or that I'm coming to see her : I want to give her a real surprise. . . . I'll take this track. — So long !' and, whispering these last few words, the wolf pattered off at a great rate into the undergrowth.

Red Ridinghood continued along her same path, but soon she saw some berries and stopped to pick them, knotting them in a cloth that was folded up at the bottom of her basket — in fact, she began to dawdle in the manner her mother had so often expressly warned her against, stopping, too, to examine the numerous funguses, in their damp but brilliant hues, scarlet or blue or purple, or in unobtrusive mackintosh shades arranged in their circles like miniature Stonehenges gone soft and spongy. . . . At last she reached her grandmother's, but no sign did she find outside of the friendly wolf, whose very existence had passed out of her mind, but whom she now suddenly recalled. . . . He must, after all, have taken a longer path, she supposed. . . . In spite of her promise,

she could not go on waiting outside : she had taken so
many hours on her way that the air was already chilly
with a foretaste of evening — besides, perhaps after all
he could not come — and she must deliver the butter
and custard, and return home almost at once, or her
mother would be very angry with her ; so she knocked
at the door.

'Come in ! Come in ! Is it you, dear child ?' the
old lady cried eagerly. Little Red Ridinghood wondered
how she could know who it was, but she lifted the latch
and entered : she could not, however, help being taken
aback by the change that a brief illness of two or three
days' duration had wrought in the old lady's voice and
appearance, in fact, in her whole personality. She had
always spoken so softly, but now every word she pronounced seemed to have a rough and furry edge, and
each sentence ended in a kind of howl. She must
certainly have been very sick. Everything about her had
always been dainty and gracious — she had retained her
pink-and-white skin, which was set off by her white hair,
like silk, and by her cornflower-blue eyes, which smiled
perpetually with a kind and cheerful look. The old lady
was sitting up in bed, wearing, as she always did on
such occasions, a rather elaborate nightdress and an old-
fashioned cap. Today, however, though the effect was
still that of a Gainsborough portrait, it was of a Gainsborough portrait gone crazy. Two pointed, furry ears
protruded from the mob-cap ; her nose, with a sort of
black leather substance at the end, round the nostrils, had

grown furry too, and her teeth, long yellow fangs where formerly had smiled impeccable dentures, did not seem, set as they were in an expression of welcome, to match the wild and ravenous dark eyes.

'Let me kiss you, dear child,' the old lady howled.

Little Red Ridinghood advanced towards the bed, and in doing so, had to step, she noticed, over a neat pile of bones, picked clean.

'Grandmother,' she explained, 'I've brought you a custard and a pot of butter from Mama, and here is a cloth full of berries that I gathered for you on the way — that's why I'm rather late in getting here. I hope——'

'I like late dinners,' her grandmother interrupted.

'I hope,' Red Ridinghood proceeded, 'that you are better. But you must be, for I see by the bones on the floor,' and she pointed at them, 'that you've been making broth.'

Now that she was near, and looked at her grandmother more attentively, she became bewildered, and, completely forgetting her mother's injunctions, exclaimed :

'Grandmother, what great ears you have !'

'The better to hear you with, my darling.'

'Grandmother, what great eyes you have !'

'The better to see you with, my precious morsel.'

'Grandmother, what great legs you have !' little Red Ridinghood continued, somewhat unwisely, in her unsolicited litany.

'The better to run after you with, dear child.'

'Grandmother, what great teeth you have !'

'The better to bite you with, my sweet,' the wolf said. 'Your grandmother, whose bones you saw, was only an appetiser — and one more thing,' he continued, with his mouth rather full, 'let your fate teach you not to make personal remarks.' Saying these words, the wolf grasped Little Red Ridinghood firmly in his paws, and began to devour her.

Beauty and the Beast

In the age in which Robert Tidcombe lived, it was not so unusual to be a rich man as it is today : to the contrary, where he resided, in Bristol, his reputed wealth caused him to be treated almost with veneration. He gained respect, too, by filling the post of churchwarden and by the variety and profusion of his charities, and lost it again by a fund of dubious stories — no, dubious is not the right word, for no uncertainty was involved ; they were frank enough to have shocked a schoolboy — by a fund, then, of dirty stories which he kept for the edification of members of his club. While in many ways he was an ordinary man, he differed, however, from most of his contemporaries of an equal social status in being the father of a large number of sons and daughters in whom he found both the chief interest and the principal irritation of his life. This family — almost a pack — consisted of seven sons and seven daughters, ranging in age between thirty-two and twelve, and since within the limited boundaries of a fairy story it would be impossible to give life to all his fourteen children, I here produce their names as a guide and indication to the reader. Drawn up in order of seniority, they read as follows :

Torfrida Gertrude (known as Cuckoo)	George Golightly
	Frederick Fretwell
Leonora Augusta	Henry Hubbard Tilyard
June Semiramis	Charles St. John
Shirley	Humphrey
Muriel Maud	Peter Peddlecock
Beatrice	Simon
Perdita Helen	

It may be fairer to add that the unassuming names were chosen by Mr. Tidcombe, the pretentious, or near-pretentious, by Mrs. Tidcombe, who had suffered all her life — and made others suffer too — because she had been christened *Queenie*.

Mr. Tidcombe was fond of all his children, but felt an especial affinity with Beatrice — or Beauty, the pet name by which she was called in her family circle. Indeed, there could be no denying that she was the most attractive of Mr. Tidcombe's children, unusually charming as well as exceedingly pretty. Her figure was tall and slight, her hair of a peculiar tarnished gold, and her skin of a flushed but delicate white : in addition even her move-ments and the gestures of her hands possessed a very definite individuality. Her character accorded with her appearance, so that even her mother — who always found it easy to spot any imperfections in friend or relation — of her was wont to say, 'Beauty has no fault except un-punctuality.' . . . Here a word must be added about Mrs. Tidcombe : a large, florid woman who looked, her friends said, 'kindness itself' : an effect she obtained by the use of pints of peroxide, and many jars of rouge

and cylinders of lipstick, and with the further aid of a
blatant voice. Like the American autumn, she contrived
to give a false impression of cheerfulness by violence of
colour. But while in public she laughed too long, too
often and too loud, on the contrary, at home she was
given to evil prophecy and to repining. For many years
now she had been foretelling to her children the approaching downfall of Mr. Tidcombe, saying to them, 'Your
father gets little enough for his money now, and mark my
words, before long we shall all be penniless.'

In fact, Mr. Tidcombe appeared to be a man unusually
fortunate in business. He had built up a small line of
boats plying between Bristol and Rio de Janeiro : (this
fleet numbered fifteen ships, and he planned to leave in
his will one vessel each to his wife and fourteen children).
He found much pleasure in his professional activities,
and outside these and the lives of his sons and daughters
his interests were few. He seldom went away, but very
occasionally he would take himself and his family for a
pleasure-cruise on one of his own ships. For his recrea-
tion he liked most of all to remain in Bristol and, as he
so deplorably phrased it, to 'exchange yarns' with the
fellow members of his club. He still occupied an old-
fashioned mansion in the city, and had not even moved
so far as Clifton, let alone London — but then he entertained no social ambitions : whereas his wife pined for
a life of visionary grandeur in the capital. But, since
it was quite plain that these longings would never be
gratified, she joined with the children at the time of

I

which I am writing in plaguing Mr. Tidcombe to take
the whole fifteen of them to London in June for a vaca-
tion. To their entreaties he finally acceded, booking for
their accommodation a few suites at the Cumberland
Hotel. Himself even began to grow excited about the
approaching visit : for though he harboured no desire to
live in the capital, he retained the rich provincial's
interest in it and respect for it. Indeed so much did he
look forward to this break of ten days in the metropolis
that in the weeks immediately preceding it he forgot
that the insurance premiums on his ships and warehouses
fell due the very morning he was to leave Bristol, and
since he had lately — already he regretted it — dis-
missed Higgins, his confidential clerk, nobody reminded
him of the fact, and the sums remained unpaid.

Until the last evening of their holiday, everything
went off well. Each member of the family did what he
or she wanted and in consequence there were fewer
quarrels than usual, and even Mrs. Tidcombe's temper
held out against the wearing gaieties in which she had
involved herself. They were leaving on Tuesday morning, and on Monday night they were all dining together
at a rather early hour before going in a body to see the
latest musical-comedy success, entitled *If a Man and a
Maid*, when there occurred the most famous storm in
history, known to us of a later era as The Great Blast, a
phenomenon unrelated in its violence to any catastrophe
of the remembered past.

The day had been fine, but ordinary enough, and

there had been few clouds in the sky. Though it was
hot outside, the dining-room was cool as a tomb, being
air-conditioned. One moment everything was quiet,
except for the hotel band which was playing with great
feeling the waltz from *If a Man and a Maid* — the next,
not a note could be heard. Doors and windows slammed,
and were then blown in, or off their hinges ; and over
the whole city there sounded at first the crash, jingle
and splinter of breaking glass. But soon the tempo
mounted, soon roofs sped through the upper air like
witches on broomsticks, avalanches of slates cascaded
down on the streets, steeples first tottered and then col-
lapsed and trees from the parks were uprooted and blown
like twigs into the whistling, screaming torment of the
air. Nor were these ravages confined to London — in
the country at large, houses were wrecked : indeed
whole towns lost every roof. The radio services were in
chaos, and there was no news, for all methods of communication were severed. But it was known that all
the continents had been gripped simultaneously by the
Great Blast. On the sea, vast boats were hurled about
like match-sticks, ships were said to have been sunk by
the hundred, and harbours to have been inundated and
washed away. This fantastic storm, which people began
to think would never end, continued for ten days :
during which, if you were lucky enough to be indoors —
and nearly every building had by this time involuntarily
become out-of-doors —, it was impossible to leave
shelter. In consequence, all business was suspended.

The Cumberland Hotel, being stoutly built, survived, but within its hospitable precincts Mr. Tidcombe could hear neither himself nor Mrs. Tidcombe speak — this last a contingency for which — though he had never foreseen it — he was profoundly grateful.

The tempest ceased as suddenly as it began. . . . It would be a matter of months before the railway service could return to normal. But two days after it had stopped Mr. Tidcombe caught one of the first trains to leave London for Bristol ; and within a week he knew the full extent of his personal share in the disaster that had fallen on the world ; indeed within a few hours he had heard enough to know that he was returning to the ruins of his home a ruined man. Twelve of his ships had been sunk, and his warehouses, and even his home in Bristol, had been burnt, because the great force of the wind had acted like a gigantic bellows, ever fanning the embers to new life once the fire had started. The Insurance Companies — recently nationalised, unified and now for the sake of simplicity and easy memorisation renamed *BIFCTUNMYRXZO* — pleaded an Act of God as their excuse for not paying for his house, while in any case they were able to refuse to compensate him for his ships and warehouses on the reasonable grounds that he had omitted to pay the premiums when they fell due. Mr. Tidcombe brought an action against *BIFCTUNMYRXZO* to claim the cost of rebuilding his mansion, but he lost. The judgement in the case was given against him and the jury added as a rider to their verdict that it was not clear to them why a rich man should expect or deserve to obtain larger damages for the destruction of his property, or of the business he had built up, than should a poor man. In addition to these ordinary misfortunes, the merchants whose goods had been stored, and burned, in his warehouses now sued him for the damage and in every instance won their cases, so that he was obliged, in order to pay, to go out of business. . . . As he was nearly sixty years of age, it seemed to him hopeless to try and start all over again, even if he could have borrowed the money necessary to begin. . . . But all this by the way — he returned, I was telling you, to Bristol a ruined man, only sustained by his beliefs. Now the religious and puritanical side of his nature asserted itself. He became convinced that his recent misfortunes were the reward of years of sinfulness and luxurious living and that in future he and his family must lead a simple existence — even simpler, indeed, than his circumstances would inevitably entail. So, as soon as he could collect his few remaining belongings, and those of Queenie and the children, and as soon as a roof could be fixed on it again, he moved to a small, grim, stone house, part farm, part cottage, which he was able to buy cheaply, and which was situated on the lower slopes of a remote mountain in Monmouthshire.

During the weeks of preparation for this change, and of installation, Mrs. Tidcombe never ceased from repining, and, more particularly, from reproaching her husband. It was his fault, entirely his fault, that the house

had been burnt down ; she had never wanted to go on
that ridiculous jaunt to London. Indeed, she now
alleged that she had warned him, prophesying that it
would end badly. The children supported their mother
in her role of Cassandra justified, and quarrelled bitterly,
too, among themselves — all except Beauty, who continued to show for her father a natural affection and
respect. No wonder, then, that she was his confirmed
favourite : she continued to remain cheerful, helped him
to organise the communal life and tried to lighten for
everyone its daily tasks. Only the long winters, wrapped
in clouds or snowbound, tested her patience, especially
when her brothers and sisters talked all day long of
former pleasure-cruises in the tropics or of winter-sports.
Their new home, where they were obliged to perform
the housework and look after the garden themselves,
was not at all to their liking ; nor did they care for the
pastoral style in which they were now compelled to
live : for they existed chiefly on the eggs from their
hens, the honey from their hives, the milk from their
cows, the vegetables and fruit from their garden, the
blueberries from the mountains. Even Peter, who was
only fourteen years of age, would attack his father
furiously, saying, 'Where is the ship you used to promise
me ?' and the rest of the family, like a chorus, would
echo his angry demands. But Mr. Tidcombe, despite
their accusations and even their threats, found in the new
way of living a curious sense of peace. When Mrs.
Tidcombe grumbled at him, he would reply :

'I feel fit, have no worries and have never eaten so well in my life.' Moreover, he slept better than usual — no doubt because the food he consumed was less in quantity and plainer : because a regular diet of rich and indigestible food is as much a stimulant to the brain, and scarcely less injurious to it, than over-indulgence in alcohol or drugs, and *pâté de foie gras* has been responsible for as many wild and highly coloured dreams as whisky or opium.

After two years of this existence, frugal and isolated, had passed, so that, to those who led it, sometimes it seemed as if only ten days had gone by since their fatal stay in London, sometimes as if two decades had elapsed, Mr. Tidcombe received news that the hulk of one of his lost ships had been located off the coast of Brazil, and that it might be possible to salvage it and part of the cargo. Now that long months of almost penitential living had allayed somewhat his sense of guilt, and also helped him to save a little money, Mr. Tidcombe had begun to feel in a less dour and a more enterprising mood, and he all at once decided to fly to Rio and see for himself what could be done. His wife and children supported this project, first because it would get him out of the house for a considerable time, and secondly because he might bring back to them some presents. Mrs. Tidcombe asserted, without being asked, that she had not the heart for jewels since that day when, with no warning, she had been forced to sell her own — but then, she did

not *like* Brazilian diamonds, which to her hardly counted
as diamonds at all, and so, in spite of everything she had
suffered, she might be persuaded to accept some. The
children demanded dresses, shawls, motor-cars and
cycles, candy, television sets and alligator-skin shoes.
Only Beauty asked for nothing, and when her father
pressed her to name a gift, said, 'Only bring me back
my favourite flower, a red rose', for since it was the
bitter core of winter in England, she would not in the
ordinary course see one for many months.

When Mr. Tidcombe arrived in Rio he found almost
immediately that the hulk was worthless, and what remained intact of the cargo had, as the compradors somewhat equivocally remarked, 'been taken by sharks.' All
he could collect was a small sum of money, just enough
to pay his expenses, and to enable him to return, travelling
steerage, on one of the ships that had formerly belonged
to him : so it was no wonder that he became depressed.
. . . On the day of his departure, he finished his packing
— what little of it there was to do — and determined to
obtain a breath of country air before sailing. He had
plenty of time, for it was now nearly four in the afternoon, and he need not be on board till midnight. A
walk would do him good, he was certain, for the tropical
glitter of this city of black glass towers and undulating
screens and vitreous green oblongs standing on their
narrow ends and springing from their angular grey-green
groves of aloe and prickly pear that seemed to have been
arrested in the very act of some significant gesticulation,

and even the perpetual sunshine in which the buildings
were washed, only made him realise his loneliness out
here. . . . He was not sure of the way, for he had not
been able to obtain a map, but it was, he supposed, only
necessary to go in the opposite direction from the sea
to reach the country. Lulled by the rhythm of his walk,
he did not, after a time, pay much attention to his
immediate surroundings : for his mind was occupied
with other things. He recollected that so far he had
been unable to buy anything for Queenie or the children.
He disliked having to return home empty-handed but it
was improbable that he would have time now to find
them presents ; he certainly would not have the money ;
and he went on to picture to himself the sort of reception
he would encounter from them all — all except Beauty,
who was as kind and good as she was lovely.

It was still very hot, but since his long tramps in the
mountains of Monmouthshire had accustomed him to
endure for miles without feeling tired, he walked on and
on, pondering the sad change in his fortunes, until suddenly he realised that he must have strayed farther than
he had intended. The sleek, flashing towers and twisting
of glass, the nests of trim but dusky millionaires with
faces from ancient Egypt, and equally the shacks made of
planks and old petrol tins, patched in places with card-
board, in which the negroes lived on the edge of the city,
all these he had left behind a long while. He tried to
reckon the time, but albeit he could tell from the position
of the sun that it was late in the day, he could not be

certain of the precise hour, for he had been obliged to sell his watch to help pay for the fare to take him home. (Queenie, who had given it to him, would find out, he was sure, and he would never till death hear the last of it !)   He now became afraid of missing the boat — but there was nothing to be done about it —, because even if he had been able to speak Portuguese, there was nobody of whom to ask the way.   He began, however, to look round him more carefully — well, it might be all very well in its way, but it was not *his* idea of *country*, he thought to himself, altogether too tawdry and ostentatious, with none of the Cotswold charm or the Monmouthshire grandeur.   You could almost see the plants growing here in this steaming heat.   It must, he concluded from its aspect, be near the Amazonian Jungle.   Under the enormous trees, tufted with epiphytes, each branch bearing a whole nurseryman's experimental table, and roped together, either with huge serpents or with the green and brown arms of the liana, it would be easy to stumble, fall and be held down till you died in the grip of this submerged green world.   And some of his gardening friends had told him — it might have been only their joke, he never could be sure — that there were orchids which ate you, when once they had got you down.   He surveyed these strange plants with disgust : (they did not look *natural*, and they weren't a patch on a wood full of bluebells).   He almost needed a matchet to hack his way through ; but what worried him most was that it was rapidly becoming impossible either to go on or to turn back. After all, though, he comforted himself, he could not have been out altogether for more than an hour and a half or two hours, and so he must still be in the neighbourhood of one of the greatest of modern cities ; nothing much could go wrong. All the same, he blamed himself for being so absent-minded and deeply sunk in self-pity that he had paid such scant regard to direction. Even the dim, almost oceanic illumination that filtered through the teeming green world above him, seemed now to be failing. . . . He was beginning to be seriously worried when he came all at once on a path, crossing his track at an angle, that looked as if it were used frequently. It lay like a streak of light across the darkness. . . . After a moment he decided that though it did not appear to lead him back into the city, his wisest course would be to follow it : for it must take him somewhere, and he would be able perhaps to find a conveyance.

A narrow cleft in the tree-tops above the path let the diminishing light in, and he could not but be amazed by the richness of jungle life, though it still shocked and — if he had admitted it to himself — rather frightened him ; he noticed, for example, the clamour, so different from the haunted silence of an English wood, the various layers of sound from monkeys, parrots and insects whose usual murmur, now magnified by their numbers, became a roar. . . . As he stopped to listen, he observed that the scene had begun indefinably to alter. It was here, on this path, as if order were gradually in course of

being imposed upon the wild profusion of Amazonian
nature. Soon the process became more evident until,
after about a quarter of an hour, he found himself proceeding up a long drive between a double avenue of
palm-trees. Apart from the exoticism of plant and tree
life, he might have been walking through a country
estate in England or France : but here the hedges were
of agave instead of hawthorn, the plantations of palm
and hibiscus, with their fragile, flamboyant trumpets of
red or yellow, and of the solandra, a shrub which bears
a huge bud, plump and closed like a fuchsia bud, but
which, if you pinch it — as Mr. Tidcombe could not
refrain from doing in one instance — gives no mere
small pop, but a hoot like that of a motor horn. . . . At
the end of the long drive stood a dignified house of two
storeys — the French, he supposed, would call it a
château —, very large, with a high roof of red tiles ; a
house, he thought, that looked as if it might have come
out of one of Hans Andersen's fairy tales, and yet seemed
strangely congruous here. It had an air of being lived
in. It would be best for him, he thought, to make his
way there, — for one thing, the walking was easier and
he had begun to feel tired — and to ring and ask where
he was and whether he could hire a motor-car in the
neighbourhood to take him back to Rio. (He would
have to find the money somehow, even if it meant
unpacking and selling a suit.)

He rang : the door opened. He entered, and it shut
behind him. He found himself in a small hall. No one

was in it, but a door led into a farther room, and Mr.
Tidcombe concluded that there must be a shortage of
servants in Brazil, too, and whoever it might be who
lived here wanted him to go on, through the door.
He knocked rather timidly, and went in.   Again, he
found himself alone : this time in a very large apartment with ten tall windows.   Opposite them tapestries
hung on the walls, and between them were huge looking-
glasses in gilt frames, — very ornate and foreign, he
judged, like the three large crystal chandeliers that
depended from the ceiling.   In a way, the effect was
handsome, he admitted, but he would never want to
live here — just at that moment, the door slammed.   He
turned back to open it, but it had stuck — or had been
locked behind him.   Similarly, now that he tried them,
none of the ten French windows would open, though
he could perceive through them an enticing prospect,
a formal rose-garden.   The blooms were splendid, he
could see from here, and the beginning of a sunset gave
colour to the prickly hedges of grey-green succulents,
which did duty here for yew and box.   He walked
towards the farther door : but that, too, was fastened
against him.   In despair, he said aloud, 'It must be very
late : what time *can* it be ?' . . . As if in answer to his
question, a clock struck the hour, seven. . . . It was
growing dark, and now the light came on.   'I'm beginning to feel hungry,' he remarked to himself — and
almost at once he saw that a small round table, laid for a
meal, had been set near the window.   He sat down at it,

and food appeared on his plate without his seeing how it was served — just as he looked down on an empty plate, another would be substituted for it, or, if it was clean, another course would appear on it. He relished the food, which was strange but delicious, and the white wine and then red, though the silence, and the manner in which the dishes succeeded one another, began to get a little on his nerves. But, after all, he must not grumble. Many people in England would be only too glad to have this automatic service in their homes : (he wondered that the Labour Party had not included it in their electoral programme). He rose from the table, and, as he did so, the door at the far end of the room opened, as if for him to go out of it, and a light, at a level just below his head, conducted him to a staircase, and up it and on, to a bedroom. Since he could not get out of the house, there was nothing for him to do save accept this invisible but rather claustrophobic hospitality with a good grace. He undressed — the pyjamas placed ready for him exactly fitted —, got into bed, and began to read one of the books on the table by his side. The moment he put it down, the light went out, and he fell at once into a deep and dreamless sleep.

The next morning when he awoke he could not make out where he was. Ripples of golden light wavered through the darkness, as if coming through tall trees, the leaves of which are swept by a breeze. But while he was still trying to remember where he had slept, the shutters swung back of their own accord, and he saw

of thanks. But go he certainly must, finding the path back as well as he could : (there was still a chance that the boat might have been delayed in sailing, and if not, then he would have to go to the British Consul, and see what could be arranged). Just as he was turning back into the house, he remembered Beauty's request, and taking a penknife out of his pocket — no one would mind, he was sure — he cut one of the finest of the red roses for her. It could be kept on ice during the journey.

In the very act, he was startled to hear such a sound as had never before reached his ears ; a sound combined of grunt, growl and roar, very loud and with a feeling of rage in it. Mr. Tidcombe was so much taken aback that he dropped the rose on the grass and turned round. . . . At first he thought he must be dreaming, for he was staring straight at the Beast. The Beast was nearly nine feet high, and when he walked seemed to be rearing himself on his hind legs : he was covered all over with orange fur, like the portion of the skin of the Giant Sloth to be seen in the Natural History Museum in South Kensington, and his face resembled that of a hippopotamus, with an enormous muzzle and small, shrewd, lumpy eyes. (Had Mr. Tidcombe been a lover of Italian pictures, he would have recognised the Beast as taken from a panel of a sea-serpent painted by Piero di Cosimo). . . . The Beast roared again, and when the preliminary fanfare had finished, Mr. Tidcombe was surprised to find that the sounds settled themselves into a run of words, stressed wrongly or at will, rather in the

manner of High Bloomsbury. Moreover, what the
Beast said was much to the point.

'Excuse my asking you, Mr. Tidcombe,' he trumpeted
thickly, 'but is this the manner in which you show your
gratitude for my unusual hospitality ?'

Fortunately the erring guest was too much surprised
to feel frightened, and he had the sense to realise that the
best course open to him was to tell the truth. Accordingly, he explained to the Beast why he had taken the
rose. Mr. Tidcombe always carried a photograph of his
favourite daughter in his pocket-book, and was fond of
taking it out to show persons who had never seen her —
or as far as anyone knew, shown the slightest interest in
her — and now, to support his story, he produced it.
The Beast examined the portrait minutely, then handed
it back. He listened attentively, too, to everything
Mr. Tidcombe told him, at times giving a series of
inarticulate grunts that were difficult to interpret as
either sympathy or disapproval, but at the end he again
bellowed his way into human speech, saying :

'I understand, and forgive you, Mr. Tidcombe ; as
a father your sentiments do you credit. But you have
missed your boat and have not enough money for a
new fare. Therefore I make you an offer — if you will
undertake to persuade Beauty to come willingly to my
Palace and live in it, I will furnish you with any necessary
money, and send you home in one of my private
aircraft. You'll be there by tomorrow morning at the
latest.'

K

When Mr. Tidcombe gave his consent to this plan, it did not seem to him difficult at all, or in any way irregular, for, though he did not know much about psycho-analysis, he comprehended that the Beast, naturally enough in the circumstances, must have developed a severe inferiority complex : because he would be aware that no woman ever entered his presence without fear and repulsion, or ever left it without relief. If, then, he could prove to himself that a woman he could admire enjoyed staying with him, it would, of course, lighten this particular burden.

The rose now appeared, wrapped in damp cotton-wool, in a box made of rushes, which allowed the air to reach it : his boxes and bags were brought (how had the Beast found out where he was staying in Rio ?), and Mr. Tidcombe, after taking leave of his unusual host, started for a private airfield on the estate. . . . It was not until the machine was circling down near his house to a moor on which the pilot declared he could land, that Mr. Tidcombe began to fear that his promise to the Beast had been given without sufficient reflection, and that the whole matter might need a lot of diplomatic explanation, to Beauty as well as to her mother.

Mrs. Tidcombe and the children were amazed to see him land from the air in a luxurious private plane, and imagined that he must have made a second fortune in the few weeks he had been away. Their curiosity was still further aroused by his first words to his favourite daughter.

He handed her the box with the rose in it, remarking enigmatically :

'Here is the present you asked for, Beauty : it is a simple gift, and I paid nothing for it — but you little know what it will cost.'

At once the whole family pressed round him, demanding that he should explain what he meant, and there, beneath the dark Monmouthshire mountains, in that sharp and aromatic air, he told them of his adventure in the tropics.

After listening to his story, Beauty in no way blamed her father, but went indoors to pack, for she insisted on accompanying him to the Jungle Palace (as they began to call it, not knowing its name) at once. Her brothers and sisters were also interested, and applauded her decision. Only her mother demurred : but she had not been given the necessary time in which to prepare a real scene, so she contented herself with stating mysteriously that she would never have thought it of her husband, but that she could not say more in front of the children. It would not be suitable, she opined, and in any case, she added, she was only too well aware that nothing, nothing at all, no argument, however well founded on principles of religion or decency, would ever persuade Mr. Tidcombe to change his mind. He was lost to every consideration except that of his own comfort, and was no doubt willing to sell herself, as well as his daughter, at a price. She would never feel safe again, not even in her own little home in the mountains ! . . . With this, she burst into tears in a most accomplished manner, and rushed indoors with a tragic agility that would have done credit to a woman half her age and with twice her wits.

Mr. Tidcombe and Beauty, undeterred, walked back to the field where the plane had landed, and found the pilot still there, engaged in going carefully over the machine. Directly he saw them, he got in. They followed his example, and within a few minutes, they were soaring aloft. . . . In what seemed an unbelievably short time they had reached the clearing in the jungle from which Mr. Tidcombe had set out, but the precise position of the domain was hidden from them by a light mist. It only cleared when they were on the ground.

The motor-car which was waiting their arrival soon deposited them at the Palace. Mr. Tidcombe rang, and the door opened and shut behind them, as it had on his first visit. . . . A delicious tropical dinner was served them on the terrace in the cool of the evening : iced paw-paw, fresh turtle soup, roast saddle of iguana, with avocados and yucca petals as salad, these dishes being accompanied by appropriate wines from Chile. So both father and daughter were in good humour when in the dusk the Beast walked out from the house and joined them. He greeted Beauty respectfully, and told her to spend the next morning in filling as many boxes as she wished with gold and jewels and clothes for her family. . . . She did not like, at such short acquaintance, to take too much — but immediately she had filled a trunk, two exactly similar and containing the same objects, would appear by the side of it. . . . After dinner that night, the Beast again came out, this time to say good-bye to Mr. Tidcombe.

In the morning two planes stood ready, one to take her father home, the other to carry the presents from Beauty to her family.

Even after Beauty had got over her first melancholy due to seeing her father leave her, she still felt sad. And indeed her days were lonely now, albeit every wish of hers was granted almost before she had formulated it. It must be remembered, in addition, that she had always been used to the company of a large family, and she greatly missed them, even though she had sometimes grown weary of their quarrels and of their noise and teasing. The hours seemed long, and she passed them under the shade of a palm tree, first reading for a few minutes, and then putting down the book and wondering what her parents could be doing at this moment, and her brothers and sisters.

If she had seen them, she might have been surprised. Mrs. Tidcombe had just unpacked one of the trunks containing jewels : on the simple oak table in the dining-room were small heaps of diamonds that glittered with a blue fire, mounds of emeralds, green as the jungle they had come from, rubies that shone with a sunset flame, peridots like transparent olives, aquamarines, topaz, turquoises, amethysts with their half-mourning sheen,

and ropes of pearls in profusion. And Mrs. Tidcombe
was at work staking her claim to all the best — the
children were not to be allowed in, until she had made
a leisurely choice. During the whole time this process
occupied she never ceased from reproaching Mr. Tidcombe most bitterly.

'To think of you, Alfred, at your time of life, getting
mixed up with the White Slave Traffic. Often have I
heard of the terrors of that trade in human souls, but I
never thought to find my own husband entangled in it.
I am bitterly ashamed. (Where did I put those emeralds
down ? They were here only a moment ago !) . . . I
haven't the heart to take the things and am only doing
so in order that the children should not put two and two
together.'

'Well, most of them could never do it, even at school,'
Mr. Tidcombe irritably retorted.

'It is no moment for repartee,' Mrs. Tidcombe stated
flatly.

Meanwhile upstairs the girls had opened one of the
trunks of clothes, and were trying them on, and shoving
one another away from the large looking-glass, which
each of them tried to monopolise : while in the passage
outside the boys were hammering a gold bar, to see if
they could divide it.

Beauty, however, entertained no inkling of these
scenes : English home-life, when viewed from this
distance, seemed to her idyllic. . . . She would read
most of the day — there was a good English library in

the Palace —, even during meals. As she was by herself, she liked to dine indoors, and later of an evening the Beast, her only visitor, would walk in through a window to see her. She soon comprehended that the reason that he always tried to put off his arrival until it was dark, was so that his hideousness should not be too apparent. She noticed, too, that — the only wish of hers that was not immediately granted — if she wanted the light to go on before or during their interview, nothing happened, but that directly the Beast quitted the room, it would be illuminated with a dazzling blue whiteness. Every evening during the short time he would be with her, he always asked her how she had spent the day, whether she had enjoyed it and whether there might be anything further she wanted. Invariably, he ended his remarks by putting to her the same two questions. . . . Considering his shyness, she thought it odd that they never seemed to embarrass him.

'Do you love me, Beauty ? Will you marry me ?'

'Oh no, Beast !' was her reply, which also never changed : but she said the words sweetly though with firmness.

Perhaps because she spent such dull and lonely days, and must, even when she was not aware of it, have longed for companionship, Beauty now dreamed a great deal, and with great vividness. And in the strange company of her tortuous and incomprehensible fantasies, one recurrent dream of an apparently simpler nature was always included. Every night a Prince, handsome beyond any

man she had ever seen, came to her, and recited with an
air of warning the following lines :

> *'Try not to miss your family or your friends :*
> *Wait here until your power of judgement mends.*
> *You've given much already : now be wise,*
> *Give more ; rely not on your eyes.'*

Then this magnificent stranger would fade into the
darkness, but leave behind him his outline, etched, as it
were, in light, until it, too, gradually faded, when she
would wake up.

Such a vision, Beauty supposed, must be an instance
of what one school of psychology would term 'sleep-
compensation' : she quite agreed with that, but it yet
struck her as singular that the same dream should be
repeated every night.

Beauty now had much time for her own thoughts,
and often and for long pondered on the problem of the
Beast. . . . She liked him, as she might like an animal,
and she was grateful to him for his thoughtfulness and
for innumerable acts of kindness, but to what race or
genus was it possible to assign him ? — to none that fell
within the range of her knowledge, limited, she admitted,
though it might be. Could he be . . . ? But British
reality asserted itself again ; she was far away in the
Amazonian Jungle, with no one to whom she could talk.
The days passed, swift and unmeaning as the flight of
birds : and still she was alone in Palace and garden. No
letters ever arrived for her — indeed, now she thought
of it, she did not know the name or the postal address

of the Palace in which she was stopping. And another small grievance : now that every wish was at once granted, she could not be unpunctual — even if there had been any occasion to be unpunctual for —, because if, for instance, she said to herself in her bedroom, 'Where is my comb, I shall be late if I can't find it ?' it would be handed to her out of the void almost before she had finished the sentence.

At last her long absence from family and friends began to tell on her health. She grew so pale and depressed that the Beast observed it, even through the failing light in which he liked to conduct these interviews. Accordingly one evening he said to her :

'Beauty, what more can I do — there must be something — to make you feel happy ? . . . As it is, I see you only for a few minutes out of the twenty-four hours. Every wish of yours is satisfied almost before it is formulated. I give you everything I can think of. . . . Are you so miserable because you hate me and want to escape ?'

'No, dear Beast,' answered Beauty, 'I like you, but I've always been used to an informal life, with crowds of people — if they're only members of my family — coming and going. I even miss the quarrels that so often break out at home. Consequently, I find this lonely and luxurious existence rather difficult to lead at first — and the tropics are hard on a woman. Especially, I miss my father. If you'll let me spend two months with Daddy, I promise to return and to remain here always, if you wish it.'

The Beast consented on the spot to the plan she had
proposed. He loaded her with riches for her family, and
the only sign he gave that her words caused him any
chagrin was a hint, phrased delicately and judiciously
introduced into one of their short evening talks, that if
she did not return within the limits of the agreed period,
she might, if she really liked him, have cause to regret
her lack of punctuality, since she might come back to
find her faithful Beast dead. . . . After these few words,
which strangely impressed Beauty, he gave her a ring
and told her that when the two months had elapsed she
must turn it on her finger and say without hesitation :

'I want to go back to my Palace, and see my Beast
again.'

That night her recurrent dream took on a different
tinge. She was walking just outside the garden, at the
edge of the forest, and there in a dusty hollow beneath
a bank of flowering cactuses she found the handsome
Prince lying ill. For a moment he rallied, and re-
proached her with having left him to his death : to
which, in her dream, she answered :

'I am only going home to tell my father I am happy
here : I've promised the Beast faithfully to be back at
the end of two months. He'd die of grief if I were to
fail him, and I'd rather perish myself than cause him
pain.'

With these words still on her lips, she woke up — in
her bedroom at her home in Monmouthshire. . . . As
the day wore on, she comprehended how greatly the

life there, and the atmosphere in the house, had changed :
because the family was prosperous again — on the riches
her father had brought back from the Beast : (all the
articles came into the country free of purchase tax and
without paying duty on them). Moreover, since she
had been away for over a year, her brothers and sisters
had in the meantime developed new interests, so that
though they tried unsuccessfully to hide it, her presence
in the house was to them at first equivalent to having a
stranger to stay. They were, however, kind and polite,
for they now recognised in her a benefactor, and they
tried to put up a show of grief when she informed them
that she had only returned for a visit of eight weeks.
Mrs. Tidcombe, on the other hand, would not speak
to her at all for several days, but after about a week
relented sufficiently to say with a shiver, and to no one
in particular :

'Ever since that fatal moment when I consented to
accept those diamonds, I've felt tainted !'

Never, though, did she offer to give back the jewels :
a discrepancy which a little shocked Beauty. Further,
when her mother saw the sables, ermine and chinchilla
her daughter had brought with her, Mrs. Tidcombe condemned them, for once rightly, as unsuited to life in the
country. She also referred to them, in front of Beauty,
as 'the price of sin'. But after a few days had passed,
and she had found that sitting by herself, shivering icily,
brought her no attention, she essayed, more successfully,
another line, by weeping continuously and saying :

'Has my erring daughter come back to me, after all ?
. . . She will always find forgiveness from Mummy.'

And, finally, when all the presents were laid out, and
Mrs. Tidcombe was able to examine them, and to realise
how fabulously valuable the gifts were, including, as they
did, tiaras and clips designed for her by the Beast himself, she thought it wiser to come in on the deal, and
though she continued in her heart to believe in Beauty's
guilt, she pretended in public to make little of it.

Alone of the family, Beauty's father was sympathetic
and understanding. He too felt sorry for the Beast.
And Beauty was able to talk to him of her daily life as
she led it in the Palace, and even to relate to him her
dreams — he was old-fashioned enough not to mind —,
describing to him how every night a handsome young
Prince materialised in her room in a most life-like
manner and begged her not to trust appearances, and
how very much puzzled she was to find a meaning to
fit this recurrent incident in her sleep. Her father considered the matter carefully, and then said to her : 'In
my opinion, the Prince wants you to understand that
you ought to reward the Beast's kindness and faithfulness
by accepting his continual proposals of marriage.'

Her family in the meantime were gradually growing
accustomed to Beauty being with them again, and their
companionship made the weeks pass pleasantly enough
— so pleasantly, indeed, that being by nature unpunctual,
as we know, she forgot that the two months of her
holiday were over, until she suddenly remembered it

one morning, after a painful dream in which she saw
the Beast dying alone in a cave.   Shocked by this into
realisation of her forgetfulness, she immediately turned
the ring on her finger, and wished to be back at the
Jungle Palace : as she did so, she fell into a peaceful
sleep and was woken — it seemed at once — by the
Palace clock calling 'Beauty !' twelve times.

All through the rest of the day Beauty looked forward to the Beast's vespertine visit : but when the
colours of the sunset died into dusk, and dusk into
darkness, still he had not made his usual appearance.
Alone as she was, she became alarmed for him — some
instinct that all was not well with him had distressed
her all day —, and though she could not see her way,
and had never before ventured further into the grounds
than the rose-garden, she went out into the darkness to
search for him.   Fortunately a magnificent full moon
appeared over the horizon, and this greatly helped her
to find the paths. . . . High and low she hunted, but
could not discover a trace of the Beast, until at last,
under a hill at the edge of the jungle, she saw him lying
in the same cave which she had seen in her dream, but
the very existence of which had been unknown to her
until tonight.   She hastened to fetch water in her cupped
hands from a fountain near by, for she could not rouse
him and feared he was dead.   She splashed the drops on
his forehead and face, but this did not revive him.   Distracted, and not knowing what to do next, she sat by
his side, stroked his head and murmured :

'Dear, *dear* Beast, I never knew how much I loved you, until now, when it is too late to tell you ! . . . What shall I do, what shall I do ?'

As she softly pronounced these words, the Beast stirred, and she could then hear that he was breathing. Within a few moments he had come to, and she was able to help him get up, and aid him on his way home. At the door he parted from her.

The next evening at dusk he paid her his usual visit and asked his customary questions :

'Do you love me, Beauty ?   Will you marry me ?'

'Yes, dear Beast,' she replied.

At this answer, there roared out a salute of twenty-one guns — the first made them both jump — and from near by fireworks leapt and soared, leaving gold lines to streak the horizon, and rich showers of gold to fall or dissolve in the night sky.   Beauty watched them for a moment, reflecting how even the fireworks here seemed to share in the gaudy profusion of the tropics, then she turned to speak to the Beast — but in place of her grotesque and furry friend stood the Prince she had seen so often in her dreams.

Now the gardens were suddenly drenched in a scintillant, diamantine light, such as is used in television, and Beauty saw approaching her two women, one dark, one fair.   The fair-haired lady led her companion to-wards the young couple, and said in the resonant, alluring tones of a film announcer introducing a trailer :

'This is Beauty, who has forced your son to abandon

his disguise in order to win her.' She added, rather un-
necessarily and with an air of declamation : 'They love
one another.'

Then, addressing Beauty, she pointed at the dark lady
and said : 'This, dear, is your future mother-in-law,
the magical ex-Empress of the Andes. You have been
staying in her enchanted Palace, with her son, the Duke
of Pernambuco. Though he is in private life a very
rich Prince, he is better known to cinema audiences over
the whole civilised world as the most famous of all
Hollywood and television stars today, Holland Clinker.
(The publicity people at Hollywood don't yet realise his
identity, though they suspect that he may be a fairy.)
In order to feel at home in the role he was to play, he
was told by the producer to spend a year in his disguise
before rehearsals started. *Minotaur*, the latest Hollywood
enterprise on the three-dimensional screen, is a story of
love and life in colourful old Crete, produced by Bethel
Montague, directed by—' but suddenly she broke off,
remembering where she was, and added : 'The Prince
will secure for you the part of the Tribute Maiden from
Greece in the same film, and you will be married to him
for a year. Then you will part, find new romances and
continue to marry happily ever after.'

Puss-in-Boots

PUSS-IN-BOOTS presented a very different outward aspect and character from those of his famous rival in the pantomime world. Dick Whittington's cat was black but comely, and had inherited something of the beauty of a famous Persian grandmother. She was all unconscious charm, all simple grace, and everything about her pleaded for affection : whereas Puss-in-Boots was sure of his abilities, and took risks that were only justifiable because the results prospered his schemes. Dick's cat was an obedient cat — that is, in so far as any cat can be obedient —, Puss-in-Boots was a commanding cat, an enterprising cat, a worldly cat, too, and ambitious, though no more for himself than for his master, but nobody could have called him a beautiful cat ; he was — I must, alas, use French words (a practice I usually condemn) to describe the effect he made, so foreign was it — he was rather *rastaquouère*, full of *espièglerie* and sparkle, with his flashy coat of pale tortoise-shell and grey, with a white, a coruscating white, front, a white mask, and with a ringed tail, somewhat like that of a marmoset : he looked as if he were pleased with his appearance, and spent an inordinate amount of time in washing. In one respect alone was he disappointed with his physical

features, his plebeian paws, which he always tried to
hide, and used often to conceal in grey velvet boots.
This led to a certain amount of criticism in the cat
world, and amusement in the human, and was responsible
for his nickname. Cats complained that he gave himself
airs, while people described him as 'quaint'. Neither
recognised his talents. . . . I have said that he was a
worldly cat, but there was one exception to this characteristic, one matter in which he remained unsophisti-
cated ; he just could not comprehend that men and
women did not appreciate being presented with the head
of a newly killed mouse. To Constantine, his master, it
was his habit to bring it, as if he, Puss-in-Boots, were a
matador at a bull-fight dedicating a bull's head to a single
favourite in the arena : he would wait, as it were, for the
applause that should greet his gesture, but never came.

Puss-in-Boots had entered the life of the young
miller by jumping through the open window, and landing on his new master's lap as if that were a usual thing
to do. Constantine never found out where he had come
from or any details of his early life. At first Puss-in-
Boots merely visited Constantine, presumably to see
how the young miller, who had lately lost both parents,
was faring, but he soon moved in altogether. He
seemed, indeed, in spite of his cleverness, to lack all
powers of concentration, playing a hundred difficult but
delightful tricks, giving a display of shadow-boxing with
some invisible insect, a moth perhaps, and even turning
double somersaults within the space of a minute to

L

divert his lonely master, who worked all day at the mill, and then returned, tired, his face and clothes powdered white with flour, to an empty house, which, though he loved it and the peace it exhaled, — an old stone cottage, existing in its own watery world, with its own typical fragrance of meadowsweet, iris and mint, and its own rhythm of falling waters — could seem desolate.

Constantine could never forget the first occasion on which the cat spoke : he had come into the kitchen in a state of exhaustion from his work at the mill ; he had wondered where Puss-in-Boots could be — for it was dusk outside and the cat was generally in by that time, so he left the door ajar, and shut the middle drawer of a chest of drawers which, for some reason or other, was open : then he had thrown himself into a shabby, old-fashioned armchair and had evidently fallen asleep. . . . When he woke, it was very dark, and he heard a clamorous, desperate sound of mewing. He at once lighted a tallow candle and looked round. The plaintive cries seemed to issue from the chest of drawers, and there soon followed a tremendous sound of banging and bumping and rustling, apparently coming from the second drawer, which he remembered shutting before he had fallen asleep. He opened it, and out of it leapt gaily the dapper cat, all troubles forgotten. In mid-air he turned towards his master and remarked appropriately :

'I know I'm not out of the top drawer, but I can certainly help you, though I'm only a common cat !'

In after years Constantine was to think how characteristic of his cat's way of speaking was this first
sentence, for the cat had a great fund of the most unpleasant slang a year or two past its prime, while otherwise
inclined to indulge a taste for an histrionic and stilted
phraseology. Yet the little animal spoke so naturally, so
much in his own personal character, that his master at
the time did not realise the new development. From
the floor the cat added, 'You don't make enough of
yourself, but I'll show you ! ' . . . And indeed from
the moment Puss-in-Boots took over, life became easier
for his master. The cat would, for example, bring him
his dinner, and fetch him if he were wanted, and generally
act as messenger, manager and aide-de-camp at the same
time. . . . At first he would not talk out-of-doors for
fear of sounding awkward and, Constantine supposed, of
being laughed at, — had there been anyone to laugh ;
since in reality day after day would pass without their
seeing a soul. . . . But no, Puss-in-Boots would only
speak at present when securely inside the cottage —
preferably, it seemed, if Constantine had fallen asleep
for a minute or two. Then the cat would turn into a
positive chatterbox.

One morning, while his master still slept, the cat, as
usual, laid the table and prepared breakfast : (for himself
he was content with a saucer of milk). He then ran
softly to an outhouse, took an old sack he had seen lying
there, and a piece of rope, plucked some tender lettuce
in the garden, and made off in the direction of the nearest

wood. When he reached it, he chose a stone of the right size, and with the materials to hand — or should I write 'to paw'? — he next fashioned a simple kind of trap, baited with the fresh green leaves. Then he hid himself in a tangle of bryony and waited, ready to let go of the rope directly any game ventured to approach the sack. . . . Presently, a fearless young leveret came near out of greed and curiosity, and the cat quickly captured him. . . . By now it was almost nine o'clock in the morning and Puss-in-Boots set off for the Royal Persian Pavilion, a palace some five miles away, in which the old widowed King Dodon held his court in great pomp and state. The distance only took the cat an hour to traverse, albeit he had on the way to dart up a tree, still carrying his sack, while a large hunting dog bounded about beneath, barking ferociously : fortunately the animal became bored after a few minutes, aware as he was that he could not climb the tree and that the cat would not come down, so he hurried on towards the wood, barking to himself and pretending that he had not noticed Puss-in-Boots spitting at him from the safety of the leafy fortress. The cat was able soon to resume his self-ordained errand. Arriving at the Palace gates, he walked straight past the sentry, entered the main door and addressed the chief page on duty, saying in a rather imperious manner :

'I am the famous Talking Cat, Puss-in-Boots : my master, the Marquess of Carabas, has sent me here with a present for the King. Announce me at once, and take away any dogs there may be in the vicinity, as I do not wish to see them.'

The page was so astonished at the animal's conversational powers, so impressed by his cat-of-the-world air, that after leading him down endless corridors, he ushered the cat straight into the presence. . . . The King was seated at breakfast. Puss-in-Boots put down the sack — which at once began leaping about on its own — made first a high jump in the air and then a low obeisance, and said :

'May it please Your Majesty, I am the famous Talking Cat of the Marquess of Carabas. My beloved master has commanded me to pay his homage to you, Sire,' and pouncing on the sack he drew out of it his catch for the royal inspection, held it up, and added, 'This leveret I myself snared this morning in one of the woods belonging to the Marquess, and he charged me to capture it alive and to present it to Your Majesty. . . . It should be very succulent, Sire, — but I must first apologise for the way in which I talk, and then withdraw.'

The King had by now recovered his composure, which had been so much shaken by a cat speaking and by a sack jumping about by itself on the floor that his crown, which he always wore at breakfast, had twice nearly fallen off his head.

'Thank you so much,' the King replied, now thoroughly diverted. 'Tell your master I am much obliged to him, no less for the game than for sending it by his celebrated Talking Cat. . . . As for apologising for the way in which you speak, you certainly talk as well as most of my ministers, to whom I have to listen for hours on end. . . . Can you by any chance recite?'

'Only a little,' the cat answered rather shyly. 'But if Your Majesty would like me to do so, I think I *could* recite *The Charge of the Light Brigade*.' . . . The cat then sat up and declaimed his piece, indulging in a profusion of rather old-fashioned gestures with his front paws, but enunciating the verses clearly.

When the performance was finished, the King said to him: 'Thank you so much. I am very partial to recitation.'

'No. Thanking *you*, Your Majesty,' the cat interrupted deplorably.

'I shall always remember this occasion,' added the King.

At the time, Constantine knew nothing of all this, but three or four days later Puss-in-Boots told his master that he would be away the next day.

In the morning he took his sack, rope and stone and some loose grain which was lying about in a barn and set out again. Mostly he rested quietly in a golden field of stubble, and after a while contrived to snare two brace of plump young birds from a running covey of partridges. They were fit for a king — and, he added to himself rather mournfully, fit for a cat, if it came to that! The King would not miss one bird, surely. But no, he must not let go for an instant of his grand design:

thanks to your master.' The cat replied that he would
much enjoy it, whereupon the King poured out the milk
with his own hand into the royal saucer and put it down
on the floor for Puss-in-Boots to drink while the King
wrote the letter, addressing it, also in his own hand,
'*To the Marquess of Carabas*'. The clever cat, with his
legal mind, hastened home, for he realised that the style,
written in the royal hand, made authentic the title he
had invented for his master, amounting by itself to a
creation. . . . The sentry glared at him and did not
salute, but he took no notice and hurried on, for he had
overheard one of the pages say to another that the King
and his only child, the lovely Princess Eglantine, were
going for a long drive that very afternoon along the
road that ran by the river-bank and, if this were so,
they would pass quite near the mill. . . . The cat did not
impart this piece of news to his master, for he knew him
to be very shy, nor did he give him the King's letter,
albeit he had promised to deliver it personally ; because
he might need the envelope later, and he was sure that
the miller would only 'put it somewhere safe', in which
case it would never be seen again : but he urged his
master to take an afternoon off from his work and bathe
in the river, at a spot which the King must pass. By
dint of imploring Constantine to do as he asked, always
ending up with the words, 'If you follow my advice,
your fortune is made', the cat roused his master's curiosity
to such a pitch that finally Puss-in-Boots got his way.
They walked down together to the place that the cat had

chosen : where Constantine undressed and plunged into
the river. The cat then took the clothes, still powdery
white from the mill, and hid them behind a rock. A
minute after he had done this, a cavalcade could be
heard approaching, and the cat ran out, wringing his
paws and crying distractedly at the top of his voice,
just as the King was passing, 'Help ! Help ! The
Marquess of Carabas is drowning !'

Hearing once more this name by now familiar to
him, and recognising the cat, the King put his hand out
of the royal coach and signalled to stop it. He then told
four men of his cavalry escort to go to the rescue. While
they hauled Lord Carabas out of the water, the cat ran
to the King again, and informed him that during the few
minutes in which his master was in difficulties in the
water, thieves had seized the opportunity and had stolen
the sumptuous clothes that he had been wearing. Hor-
rified to hear of this new misfortune which had befallen
the young man, kindly King Dodon sent four of his
fastest cavalry back to the Palace to fetch some of his
own clothes, the most splendid in the royal wardrobe.

Arrayed in the King's robes, the young miller looked
magnificent as he came to thank his royal benefactor.
The King offered congratulations on his escape, and
invited the young man to accompany him in the coach.
He then presented the miller as the Marquess of Carabas
to Princess Eglantine, who thought him charming, so
unlike most of the men she met, and when he cast a
glance — or part of one — in her direction, a glance at

the same time bold and timid, admiring and respectful, she fell immediately in love with him.

Puss-in-Boots, enchanted at the success of his schemes so far, ran ahead. . . . Presently, he saw some peasants working in a field at the side of the road, and said to them, 'I'm a magical cat and can cast spells. If, when you are asked in a moment or two to whom this land belongs, you don't reply "To the Marquess of Carabas", I'll see that you are sliced into little pieces.'   Accordingly when, in a few minutes, the King stopped the coach, beckoned to the peasants, and asked them the very question, they answered as they had been advised.   But the young man did not hear, so full was his head of the Princess : in consequence, when the King said to him, 'You have fine possessions,' he misunderstood, and thinking that the King must be alluding to his robes, replied, 'Indeed, Sire, they are worthy of you !'

In the meantime the cat had rushed ahead, covering the ground at his own rapid but easy canter.   Soon he came upon some reapers in a cornfield, and adopting the air of command he had recently devised, said to them : 'Good people, I'm a magical cat and can cast spells, and if you don't tell the King, when he passes this way in about twenty minutes, that these fields are the property of the Marquess of Carabas, you will be turned into stone. . . . Now try it over.   When I say "To whom do these fields belong ?" you answer, after counting one, two, three, "To our beloved landlord, the Marquess of Carabas."

'To whom do these fields belong?   Now, all together, one, two, three.'

'To our beloved landlord, the Marquess of Carabas.'

'That's good ! Well, don't forget it !'

Frightened by the threats of Puss-in-Boots, the peasants decided to obey, and when, a few minutes later, the King stopped the royal coach, and enquired of them to whom the fields belonged, they answered in chorus as rehearsed.

'You are fortunate to have a fine and devoted body of men to work your estates,' the King observed to Constantine.

'All of this is new to me,' the puzzled young miller replied.

Similarly, the cat, always ahead and just out of sight, by the use of identical methods, induced the peasants to assign the ownership of woods, hop-fields, pastures, herds and orchards to the same mythical proprietor.

The invariable and flattering replies impressed the monarch.

'A fine patrimony, and plainly an excellent landlord,' exclaimed the King, turning towards the young man in congratulation.

Constantine replied : 'To my own knowledge, all I own is a partly derelict mill.'

'You are indeed a modest young man,' said the King, adding, 'it is a quality I value.'

The cat still galloped in front, until he reached the Castle of the local Ogre, to whom in reality belonged all the possessions just declared by the various groups of peasants to be the property of the Marquess of Carabas. The Ogre, of course, knew nothing of all this. The cat at once approached the guard on duty and said to him, 'I am the famous Talking Cat, and I have come to pay my respects to the Ogre.' The man lowered the drawbridge and let him in, pointing to an enormous door at the top of a flight of stone stairs.

When Puss-in-Boots entered, the Ogre was resting in an immense armchair, as large as a house. The cat made a low obeisance and then said boldly : 'I am the Talking Cat, of whom you will have heard : but you will not have heard more about me than I have about you — among other things claimed for you is one that I simply can't believe to be true ; that you can turn yourself at will into any animal you choose.'

The Ogre, annoyed at this denigration of his powers, rose up, like a mountain moving, glared at the perky newcomer and shouted furiously, 'It's true, and I'll prove it !' His words, as he finished them, became a roar, and in his place stood now a huge, tawny lion, who shook his mane and glared implacably at the cat. The cat was so genuinely alarmed that he took a flying leap on to the top of a wardrobe, tall enough to afford him protection. 'Good Heavens !' he cried, his white face just showing over the top, 'what a fright you gave me !'

The lion — that is to say the Ogre — was vastly amused at the result of his transformation upon the morale of the impudent newcomer. And though he continued to roar in an intimidating manner, his evident success made him entertain more amiable feelings towards the cat, who still remained in his refuge until, after a minute or two, the Ogre assumed once more his own shape, and shaking the whole castle with his laughter, called up, 'Now are you satisfied? You can move in safety.'

Accordingly the cat jumped down to the floor.

'Safety,' the little animal repeated, 'that is a very precious thing, even to one with my proverbial nine lives. . . . Of course, I was only alarmed because I had not expected to see anything so soon. I thought it would be a slower process.'

'Oh, of course!' the Ogre mocked, still laughing. 'But at any rate, I hope my demonstration has persuaded you that I can turn into any animal I choose, at any time I like.'

'Well, yes, into any *big* animal — for, if I may say so without offence, there is a largeness about you yourself. But I can't pretend that I can believe that you could turn yourself into a small creature, like a mouse.'

'No?' the Ogre roared. 'Just see if I can't!'

. . . The Ogre had scarcely stopped speaking when he disappeared, and his place was taken by a charming but diminutive brown mouse.

This was the culmination of the wily cat's scheming, and much as he would have liked to play, and to tickle it as if it were a trout, he took no risks, but pounced on it at once, saying to himself, 'He who laughs last laughs best.' Even in this brief incident he evinced a wonderful technical mastery, as he killed and ate it — all except the head, which for the moment he hid under the wardrobe because in his mind he reserved it for a special purpose later on.

Puss-in-Boots proceeded to run through the whole building, calling out to all the servants that the Ogre was dead, and that from now onward their master would be the Marquess of Carabas. . . . No sooner had he completed his tour of the Castle than the King's escort rode into the Great Court, followed by the royal coach. Puss-in-Boots, with a graceful and courtier-like bow, welcomed the King at the door.

'Is this yours, too, Lord Carabas ?' the King enquired of the young man.

'It is all I have,' replied Carabas, thinking the King was alluding to Puss-in-Boots.

Impressed again by the modesty of the words, the Sovereign decided that he would be the ideal husband for the Princess. . . . In the Long Hall a sumptuous meal was served. The cat, turned master of the ceremonies, bowed the King, the Princess and the miller to their places. The slain Ogre had been very fond of music, and his orchestra now played in the Minstrels' Gallery the King's favourite pieces. The food and wine were excellent, since the Ogre's kitchen and cellar lacked nothing.

The King consulted the cat on an important matter — that of selecting a new title for Constantine, since of the

old one the Heralds could find no trace. . . . That, explained the cat, was because the title was so ancient that
the deeds had fallen to dust long ago. 'But I can produce,' he added, 'an envelope addressed to the *Marquess
of Carabas* in Your Majesty's own hand, and that is tanta-
mount to a creation or at least to an authentication of the
title. In other words, Sire, it makes it O.K.' The King
agreed that this was so, and, in addition, created Constantine a Prince, so that he could marry the Princess
and, when the time came, could succeed the King on
the throne. A few weeks later the marriage was announced to take place soon between 'Our beloved
daughter Eglantine and the most puissant Prince Constantine, Marquess of Carabas' — in short, between the
young miller and the most beautiful Princess in the world.

The cat, alas, could not very well be best man at the
Royal Wedding, but he was given a seat among the
chairs placed in front of the first pew, and as a wedding
present he gave the bridegroom the head of the mouse —
formerly the Ogre — mounted on a gold shield, and he
related to his master the story of how he had secured it.

The King appointed the cat a Privy Councillor and
showered honours on him. . . . One day the King came
to him and said, 'I owe you an immense debt of gratitude
for many good deeds — not least for calling my attention
to that admirable young man, now my son-in-law and
heir to the throne. . . . Tell me, is there anything further
I can do for you ?'

'Well, Your Majesty,' the cat replied, 'nearly all of us

Bluebeard

'If I must read aloud,' I replied, 'I would rather not read the story of Bluebeard to you. After all, you've been ill and, though you are much better now, I think you would find it far too gruesome — and too old-fashioned. Such things just couldn't occur in our age. . . . You had much better let me read the paper to you ; you haven't heard any news since your illness began ten days ago. . . . Here's *The Times* for November 19th. I'll read the first paragraph that catches my eye. Now—' and I found myself reading aloud the following account of a recent discovery :

'*Ten Bodies Found on Wisconsin Farm.* Plainfield, Wisconsin, November 18th. — The remains of five more bodies were added today to five found here yesterday on the 160-acre farm of a bachelor farmer, Ed Gein. The search at the farm was continued yesterday after police found the headless body of a missing elderly woman and the skulls and bones of several other persons. Gein has been detained pending further investigation, police said.' (I found out later from other papers that cannibalism was imputed as one of the motives. The crime was therefore more utilitarian than Bluebeard's. Bluebeard did not eat his victims.)

'Well, that rather destroys my argument, I'm afraid, and now, after all, I may as well read to you the older story.'

Bluebeard was no one-girl man. Even Lucille, his final bride, knew that there had been other wives before her, but she was not aware how many there had been, nor that he was a self-made widower many times over. In every other respect Lucille had entered the state of matrimony with her eyes wide open. . . . All the same, when finally she threw back the shutters and the light flooded in, what she saw had come as a shock to her.

Ostensibly Bluebeard had many points in his favour. . . . At the time of their engagement he was a rich man and had even made money in a period of capitalist decline, though how he had amassed his fortune not even his oldest acquaintances had been able to discover ; indeed, many details concerning Bluebeard remained a little mysterious ; not least, the matter of his origin. He was now a Grudgling citizen, but he certainly had not been born one. Nor was he British or French, though he spent more time in London and Paris than elsewhere. Some of his friends believed that he hailed from Turkey in the reign of the Sultan Abdul Hamid, from whose delicate example he had learned much at an early age, and they deduced further that he had been a Pasha, had transferred some of the revenues derived from the province he had administered to Paris for greater security, and had arrived in the French metropolis in person, wearing a fez and a frock-coat, in 1906 : others said he was a magician who had posed as a Smyrna merchant. There were also questions concerning him of a more serious nature — such as what precisely had happened to his previous wives — waiting to be investigated, but nobody seemed to worry about them at the time. Though not exactly good-looking, he could have been described as a fine figure of a man. On him even his famous beard looked handsome, and in no manner *outré*. It was not a Reckitts blue, but a navy blue, and set a fashion among his new friends — or should I write 'among those new acquaintances dazzled by his wealth' ? — who now went in a body to their barbers and demanded a blue rinse for their beards . . . Only Lucille's mother, though she was in favour of the marriage, disapproved of her future son-in-law's beard : it was difficult to know why, until at last she blurted it out :

'I don't think that his beard,' Lucille had remarked to her one day, 'is nearly as blue as it's painted !'

'It's not painted, darling,' her mother replied. 'It's natural — but, all the same, *what will the neighbours say* ?'

Lucille had been able to soothe her mother and allay her fears by pointing out that her future home in Grudge-land, Bluebeard's Castle, was completely isolated and free of neighbours.

Lucille Portebouche and her mother were both French. Lucille was a model — the term is here used in the news-paper sense to denote a profession rather than as a tribute to decorum. It had been a whirlwind courtship, and both mother and daughter felt that they needed a change of air for a few days before the wedding, which was scheduled to take place in Grudgeland : (this was irregular, Madame Portebouche had reflected, but realising the economy it would mean for her — since, owing to the currency difficulties, Bluebeard had offered to pay the whole cost — she raised no objections). But now the bridegroom suddenly altered his plans and decided that the ceremony should take place in Paris at the Grudgling Church, and that the honeymoon should be spent at the Castle. Fortunately he still insisted on defraying all the expenses. However, though Madame Portebouche suffered no financial loss by the alteration, it nevertheless entailed more work for mother and daughter : in consequence they had to abandon the idea of a short pre-nuptial visit to London. . . . In a way, Lucille was relieved when they had reached this decision, for the great number of murders that had occurred in and round our foggy metropolis made French people nervous of venturing there even for a few days. Indeed, England led the world that year in murder, and could boast, too, of the largest number of mysterious killings still unsolved. Even such French champions as Landru or Gilles de Retz could scarcely compete with Christie and Haigh. But, in parenthesis, the English do not consider marriage as an essential prerequisite to murder.

The marriage, a fashionable and expensive celebration, took place. Everything went off well and Madame Portebouche and her younger daughter Anne cried to

the limit permitted by convention.   Afterwards there
were the wedding presents to see and toasts to drink
to the health and prosperity of the happy couple, who
shortly afterwards left for Bluebeard's Castle.

Lucille had never seen her husband's Grudgling home
before and was immensely impressed with its glories.   It
occupied the top of a hill, standing there as though it
were a natural feature, its immense size and the colour
of the stone from which it was built making it seem
part of the landscape.   The exterior of the Castle was
Gothic, an assembly of unconnected turrets and grey
stone walls.   On the south side a later formal garden led
down in broad terraces to a wide but deserted plain which
stretched to the horizon.   The interior of the Castle was
magnificent, full of rooms painted by the great Italian
masters, and displaying the various collections that Bluebeard had formed, of pictures, furniture, china and glass,
all of the finest quality. . . . This was a side of Bluebeard's character that Lucille had not yet fully appreciated.
In fact, Bluebeard was a very cultivated and well-read
man, as his libraries testified. . . . Yet Lucille began after
a few days to feel lonely in this grandeur — for one thing
she never saw a servant or gardener, though there could
be no complaint of the service or the flowers, but Bluebeard explained that he liked to keep the running of the
place in his own hands. . . . Lucille spent much time
wandering about the Castle, trying to comprehend the
plan of it, and to memorise its rooms and passages and
galleries, but this she found difficult.

Yes, she was lonely, because though Bluebeard was kindness itself to her, he would absent himself for hours at a time and would only excuse himself by saying, 'I had a difficult piece of work to do', — yet he never explained the nature of his occupation, and she did not like to question him ; she did not exactly know why, but some instinct warned her to refrain.

After a fortnight or so, Bluebeard informed her that professional business obliged him to go away for ten days. He would start in a week's time. . . . Perhaps he had divined her incipient loneliness, for he now suggested, since he did not wish her to be by herself, that she should ask a friend or relation to stay until his return . . . . Accordingly she wrote to her sister, who immediately accepted. Without telling her husband, Lucille also invited her two brothers, who promised to spend a night on their way to take part in an international horse show. Since they would come on horseback, it would not be easy to announce beforehand the exact hour of arrival.

Anne had already appeared when the day came for Bluebeard to leave. He had been as usual very affectionate to his wife : until, just before leaving, he summoned her to see him alone, and said :

'Here are the keys of my Castle. These three smaller ones are for the chests of gold and silver, and for the jewels, which you have not yet seen : these are the keys of the rooms — and this,' he added, carefully picking out from the rest a rather large and rusty key, 'is the only one that I absolutely forbid you to use. It opens the door of my working-room which leads out of the end of the Long Gallery. No one is ever allowed to enter, except myself. If you disobey me, I shall be aware of it, for I have an instrument of detection which is infallible, and I must warn you that the retribution would be terrible.' These words he spoke in a tone of intimidating gravity.

Lucille promised not to open the door of this chamber, and although she regarded it as rather a silly stipulation, she concealed her feelings. (After all, what secret *could* he have to guard from her?) But Bluebeard seemed satisfied by her answer, kissed her and said goodbye.

That morning Lucille spent in showing her sister over the Castle. They walked through halls with columns of amethyst, of lapis and of malachite, each with appropriate furniture inlaid with the same substance as that of the pillars and made by famous Grudgling designers. They went through the Rose Ballroom into the picture gallery, and they opened the chest of jewels. First there were ropes of pearls in wonderful condition, Lucille thought — indeed, they looked as if they had been worn frequently and recently —, trays of diamonds, emeralds, sapphires, rubies, aquamarines, peridots, jacinths, girasoles, and many other gems, some mounted splendidly, others unset. They passed some time in trying on the tiaras, necklaces and bracelets, and it was a curious sight, had anyone else been present, to watch these young women in their ordinary day clothes, wearing tiaras and covered with jewels, proceeding through the empty halls. Anne, in her own heart, felt, though the marvels of the Castle astonished her, that it was not 'home-like'. At the end of the tour, she said to Lucille :

'Darling, all the same, in spite of its beauties, it is easy to tell that for a long time no woman has presided here. It needs a woman's touch. You must take your rightful place.' Then, pointing to a door, she added :

'Where does that door lead ? . . . It's the only one you haven't unlocked.'

'That is the door of *Bluebeard's Chamber*, or as he calls it, his studio ; I've given him my solemn word not to enter it.'

As she said this, she looked rather uncomfortable, for she saw that Anne's curiosity was aroused, and her inquisitiveness was a byword in her family and among her friends, and, indeed, she now began to bully and work on Lucille in order to induce her to break her oath :

'It is your *duty as a wife* to see what that room contains. You are the equal of any man, no secret should be hidden from you.'

In the end, after receiving many such little homilies and exhortations, which in all lasted about half an hour, Lucille gave way, saying :

'I'll enter the studio on one condition — that you go up to the roof, Sister Anne, and watch the plain : because I have a curious hunch that Bluebeard may return today to find out whether I've kept my promise. . . . Call down to me if you see anyone approaching.'

Now that the matter was decided, their mood changed.

They were both young and they raced along the gallery, filling it with the patter of footsteps and with laughter. Then Anne took off the jewels she was wearing and gave them back to Lucille to put away.   Lucille remarked, 'I'll keep mine on for the present.   I like the feel of them, they give me confidence,' — and Anne climbed the little staircase to take up her position on the roof, from where she could still hear Lucille's laughter.

Lucille now stood outside the forbidden door, and selecting the key which Bluebeard had indicated, fitted it into the lock.   It turned easily, but as she was just going to open the door, she experienced the physical sensation that she had upset some liquid on her hand, and letting go of the key, she withdrew her hand from the shadow that the door seemed to cast, into the full light, and found that her hand was stained with blood. . . . She must have scratched or cut herself, she supposed, without noticing it. . . . Still, it was an odd thing to happen.   She wiped the key, which appeared to be clean, and then again grasped it.   Immediately she had the same sensation of moisture on her hand, and looking down saw that again it was covered with blood. Oh well, it was no good going on like this !   She stopped laughing and resolutely opened the door. . . . The stench of death filled the room.   She knew what it was, atavistically, though she herself had never encountered it before.   She could see nothing, because the shutters were closed.   She nearly fell — the floor seemed curiously slippery — in walking across to the window, which she flung open. The sunlight flowed in, and for a moment she was dazzled. . . . Suddenly, she saw — and it was then that she started to laugh again, but in a different way. . . . She was in a lofty vaulted room, the walls of which were lined with heads, preserved in some way and mounted on simple wooden shields, as the walls of an ancient hall might be lined with the antlered heads of stags : but in this case the heads were the heads of women. Each trophy had a name below it, on a plain wooden label, the letters incised in gold, with an accompanying date. (She noticed a spare space left for one head, with the name, *Lucille*, already on the label, though it carried as yet no date.) In the centre of the floor was an unspeakable heap of knives and limbs and ropes and hatchets and saws in bloodstained confusion : the floor itself was greasy with blood. . . . So this was the work that Bluebeard carried out with so much care and attention, and upon which he lavished so many hours ! Here were her ten predecessors, whom he undoubtedly intended her to join at the earliest possible moment. (The sound of the laughter of Bluebeard's wife, a kind of laughter in reverse, reached her sister on the roof, who wondered what the joke could possibly be. . . . Anne was right. There was a joke : that Lucille had been relieved that her visit to London was abandoned because of the many murders there, and here she was, trapped by a multiple murderer. And there was another cause for wry laughter, if she could have seen herself, standing in the bright sunlight, her jewels flashing on her day clothes, a figure of be-

wildered desolation. She knew she would never wear
them again.) . . . She hardly dared to breathe ; the
atmosphere of the whole room exhaled a sense of immediate danger ; the pattern of her footmarks was to
be seen so clearly on the floor that Bluebeard was bound
to find out about her visit the next time he entered his
'studio'. . . . The only thing that could possibly save
her and her sister would be the arrival of her two brothers
on their way south : so she stopped laughing, and going
to the door, called up :

'Is there anyone in sight, Sister Anne ?'

'Not a speck of dust as yet,' came the answer.

Lucille replied : 'I'll explain later, but I ask you to
keep in mind that our lives may depend on your watching carefully and continuously, so don't woolgather as
you sometimes do.'

Almost immediately, her sister called, 'Lucille, Lucille !
Now I can see a speck of dust. It must be a car.'

'That will be Bluebeard, then,' Lucille shouted back,
hurriedly slamming the door behind her, and locking it.
She just had time, before Bluebeard appeared, to wash
the bloodstains from her hands and to put the jewels
away. He explained that on the way he had been
handed a letter, telling him that the business for which
he was taking the journey had already been concluded
in his favour : it seemed silly to proceed further, so he
had returned home.

His wife did all she could to simulate pleasure at
his unexpected return. . . . Dinner that night was

nevertheless a grim meal. Lucille had lost her appetite: a fact that Bluebeard duly noticed. . . . And then Anne, who was usually tactful but as yet knew nothing of Lucille's discoveries, said to Bluebeard, as she watched him dismembering a roast chicken, 'How beautifully you carve ! You must have had a lot of practice.' . . . He gave her a vibrant glance, but did not respond. . . . Soon after dinner was over, Lucille and Sister Anne went upstairs, excusing themselves on the score of headaches ; and Lucille persuaded her sister to sleep in her room, and thus was able to tell her of what she had found.

So far Bluebeard had not mentioned the keys, but the next morning, as soon as she was dressed, he came in to say good morning, and at the same time asked, almost nonchalantly, for the keys, which she managed to return to him with scarcely a tremble. He took them, looked at them, and at once demanded, in a manner completely changed :

'How is it that the key of my studio is not with the others ?'

'I must have stupidly left it upstairs,' she replied.

'Go and fetch it at once,' he said, his beard looking blue-black as a thunder-cloud.

In the end, after contriving many delays, she had to give it up to him. As soon as he touched it, he said, 'There's blood on the key. Why ?'

'I can't imagine why. . . . As a matter of fact, I was just going to ask you the same question,' Lucille said, turning pale.

'You can't explain, but I can,' Bluebeard retorted ; 'my question was entirely rhetorical, and I did not expect an answer. The key is a magical key, and if any-one unauthorised unlocks the door of my sanctum, blood, which cannot be wiped off, appears on the key : thus the intrusion is revealed. Contrary to my commands, and to the oath you took, you went in. And now, as a result, you'll go in again — this time for good. You'll take your rightful place.'

Lucille threw herself at her husband's feet, imploring forgiveness. So beautiful did she look in her distraction that you would have expected the sight of her to have melted even a heart of diamond.

Bluebeard merely said, 'You must die — the sooner, the better. I will deal with your sister Anne later.'

'Since I must die,' she entreated him, her eyes holding in them the weeping of all the world, 'give me a little time in which to pray for courage and resignation.'

'Very well, Lucille,' Bluebeard at last conceded, 'you shall have a quarter of an hour, but not another moment.'

He then left the room, and after a minute Lucille went to the door and called up, just loud enough for her words to reach her sister, but not to carry to Bluebeard :

'I haven't time to explain yet, so don't waste precious minutes by asking questions. Sister Anne, Sister Anne, do you see anyone in the plain below ? . . . If you do, it will be our brothers. They said they would try to visit us on their way. When you see them, signal to them urgently to hurry — even as it is, they may be too late to help you or me.'

Lucille called up continually, 'Sister Anne, is anyone approaching ?' and the reply would come, 'I see nothing but a golden haze.'

Meanwhile the fifteen minutes that had been granted had passed, and Bluebeard shouted, 'Lucille, I'm waiting for you in my studio. Come up at once, or I'll come down and fetch you.'

'Grant me a few more minutes,' his wife besought him, and she cried again to her sister, 'Do you see anyone, Sister Anne ?'

'I see a cloud of dust.'

'It must be our brothers,' Lucille answered.

'No, Lucille, I can see clearly now ; it is a flock of sheep and a shepherd.'

'Come up this instant !' roared Bluebeard.

'I shall be with you in a minute's time,' Lucille replied.

Now Anne called down, 'I see two clouds of dust moving fast towards us.'

'God be praised ! That will be our brothers.'

'Yes, it is two horsemen. I can see them distinctly. I am doing all I can to make them gallop here as quickly as possible.'

Bluebeard's voice made itself heard again ; indeed his voice sounded so loud and angry that it seemed to shake the whole Castle. His poor wife delayed until he started to come down, carrying with him an enormous knife. He seized her by the hair, while she still implored him for a few minutes more. He began to drag and tug her upstairs, she screaming in her terror.

'Stop yelling,' he said, 'and commend your soul to God : it is no good your begging me for mercy. Your time's up' — but now there sounded a loud knocking at the Castle door, which echoed through the whole huge building. Bluebeard in his surprise let go of Lucille's hair, and the knife dropped from his other hand. The horsemen — for it was her brothers as she had foreseen — had tethered their mounts by the portcullis and now broke down the door and, guided by Lucille's cries for help, rushed upstairs, brandishing their swords. They hurled themselves on Bluebeard and bore him to the floor : they then ran him through the body with their swords. All this happened in a single instant.

I wish I could tell you that after so many shocks and so much suffering compressed into a few hours, Lucille had lived happily ever afterwards, but I cannot. The next few years were a time of long-drawn-out distress and worry for her. . . . Bluebeard left no will, so by Grudgling law all his property went to his widow. The story of his life and death filled the newspapers for a week. Then he suddenly faded out of public interest and it seemed that a period of peaceful life might be beginning : but this was not to be.

One morning, about three weeks after Bluebeard's death, the post arrived while Lucille and Anne were at breakfast. There were the usual letters of praise and of abuse ; but among the correspondence was one that bore the always welcome inscription —

Grudgling Inland Revenue Department

(A word must be written about this great national service, which had lately been incorporated into the Ministry of National Frustration : a happy combination, for the ministry had for many years grown daily in scope and power, until it now controlled the efforts, careers and lives of nearly every Grudgling — but in my enthusiasm for a great institution, I wander.) Lucille, I was explaining, had received a stout envelope, which in size resembled a parcel, having the heading I have mentioned ; and when in her excitement she tore it open, out tumbled a cascade of elaborate forms, together with a long letter. The argument which this communication advanced was unexpected but ingenious : that Blue-beard had inherited the property of each of his previous wives, on which, since their deaths had not at the time been recorded, it had been impossible up till the last week or two to put forward a claim for death duties, but that now Lucille, as ultimate heir of their estates, was clearly responsible, and their claims, they explained, were made in order to encourage saving which was essential if the nation was to survive. As a beginning it was obligatory for her to fill up in triplicate the enclosed forms giving the names of her ten predecessors, the dates of their birth and death and details of how they died, the religion or religious denomination to which each belonged, the maiden names of aunts and grandmothers, together, of course, with minutiae of their belongings — jewellery, furs and attire —, all to be given with speed and accuracy under penalty of imprisonment with torture. . . . Poor Lucille knew nothing about these women : she had been happily unconscious of the very existence of most of them until three weeks previously, — all the information she could provide being the stark and repulsive facts inscribed on the wooden labels under the mounted heads of the women in Bluebeard's studio, and somehow or other she did not fancy spending much time there at present ; besides, how was she to guarantee the authenticity even of the few facts stated there ? . . . Further, the Inland Revenue Department advanced the theory that because, for example, Bluebeard's first wife — if she were his wife, and if she were the first — had been killed some twenty years before, the death duties to be levied would include compound interest over that period on the sums owing from her estate ; and the same claim was made on the property of each subsequent wife in the order of their progression.

Lucille was for many years distracted by the whole business and could not sleep at all. Eventually, however, and contrary to expectation, the matters were settled, a compromise being reached by which the Minister of National Frustration accepted in part payment of the claims of the Grudgling Inland Revenue Bluebeard's collection of knives, scimitars, swords, axes, saws, ropes and other implements of his profession, and they were

N

removed to the new Museum of Technical Apparatus. This announcement coincided with another intimating that there had passed into public ownership on similar terms the various masterpieces of painting in Bluebeard's gallery. These official statements aroused the widest interest and led to the appearance of many hysterical letters in the daily Press. The old masters, most of them agreed, should not be removed to the Grudgling National Gallery, but should be allotted to a provincial gallery, where they would never be seen and could not be properly cared for : other letters protested that all the pictures should at once be appropriated and hung in the National Gallery, as they were 'National Treasures' — though, in fact, they had never at any time had anything to do with the nation, not even having been painted by Grudgling artists, but were the work of foreign individuals and purchased by patrons of the arts who were usually unpopular with the public, coming only second in this to the artists themselves.

Other letters demanded the immediate return of Bluebeard's collection of weapons from the Museum of Technical Apparatus to the Castle, of which they formed the chief attraction for tourists, providing, as one letter-writer phrased it, 'a rare glimpse, not only of gracious living but of gracious dying'. So high did public feeling rise over these matters that the protest was successful and the weapons were returned. . . . But I have forgotten to inform the reader that Lucille had, a month or two after the death of her husband, opened Bluebeard's

Castle to the public, who arrived in droves day after day to visit it. After Lucille had reached her settlement with the Ministry of National Frustration, she handed over Bluebeard's Castle, together with sufficient investments to support it, to the Grudgling National Trust, on condition that she should be permitted to continue to live in part of it.

All those connected with the Ministry of National Frustration and the Grudgling National Trust lived happily ever afterwards.

Dick Whittington

YOU may well enquire, child, the history and purpose of that enormous red-brick building over there : that is the famous *Whittington Central Cats' Aid Society and Sanatorium*. And, for once, I will consent to tell you its story, on condition that you do not interrupt and that if you fail to understand anything, either a word or a sentiment, you will keep your questions until the end. I do it all the more readily because it is a tale that will help to equip you for the world. In order, however, that you may derive the full benefit from the moral to be drawn, we must begin almost at the end, so that we may obtain thereby a glimpse of the glories that crowned Whittington's career, because it is essentially, in the delightful modern phrase which you would do well to ponder, a 'success-story', indicating how Perseverance and Industry are rewarded, and that we need never despair of Providence assisting us, if only, at the beginning of our lives, we learn to assist ourselves.

It was a typical November, early November, day in the City of London. All the morning the crowds had surged in the streets, as they still called the narrow traffic lanes between the camouflaged hoardings that hid the broken façades of houses and the derelict brick-strewn areas. Here and there, a stout Norman tower survived, or an opalescent belfry by Wren pricked the grey sky as it had done for three centuries, while from it sounded the accustomed peals. The excited people jostled one another, and in places the crowd was so great that it broke through the hoardings and swarmed into the bomb craters, now, by the miracles of Science, as large as Greek theatres. Throughout the morning the weather had been fine, and not *really* cold, the onlookers had said, as they thrashed their arms together and blew their noses. It only *seemed* cold, because this year the Show had taken so long a time to pass. But that was natural enough, too, and one must not grumble, for it had been designed to portray the Blessings of Peace.

As usual, the Bishops had blessed the tanks, that were wreathed with branches of olive, and in short sermons had pointed out that if men wanted peace, they must avoid being *peaceable*, must on the contrary be prepared to fight at once, to fight everyone, everywhere, and at the same time. Peace was not something negative, not just a period in which people were not making war ; it should be a period of active preparation for the next struggle. Only thus could a true peace be attained ; only thus should we make ourselves worthy of peace. . . . Then the procession started. First, on a mammoth car, came the miniature model of a bombed city — easy to make, but effective. (The onlookers cheered themselves hoarse.) Then followed bodies of flame-throwers in

masks and armour, who drew behind them on a carrier
a vast bomb, then bits of aircraft, lifted shoulder-high,
then detachments of atom-splitters and electron-smashers
in their uniforms of synthetic rubber, then platoons of
freezers in their new, non-conductive suits, inflated like
those of divers, then a car on which were placed what
the crowd for the most part held to be dummies, copied
from the enemy dead — but some maintained that this
would be too expensive, and that they were the real
thing, preserved by a new secret process — and, finally,
battalions of the new peace-keepers, as they were termed,
wound up the whole parade, their faces painted with pigs'
blood, while, for arms, they carried knives, bombs, gren-
ades, pocket machine-guns, rays and rubber truncheons.
These last were the most popular item of all, and the
crowd, especially the schoolboys in it, cheered till they
could cheer no more. But *everyone* had enjoyed the
Show. It had struck a new note, people agreed ; you
know, *modern, realistic* ; none of the old papier-mâché
stuff. Alas, as the Lord Mayor's coach, in which that
dignitary, with fur-lined robe and cocked hat, could be
seen rolling like a porpoise, neared the spectators, a drizzle
began and a little marred the pageantry.

The afternoon was wet, very wet, the rain pouring
down the folds of thousands of waterproof coats, seeming
to make of their shapes something noble, as if turning
them to stone. Lamps glowed through the yellow
darkness, and the reflecting surfaces of wet broken
stone, wet broken tarmac, wet broken cement, showed

an infinity of watery lights. The faces of the newspaper boys, as they dashed along the pavements, were turned at that angle towards the sky at which the faces of figure-heads are set, and were varnished with the rain.

'*Lord Mayor's Banquet, Sensation !*' they were crying. The eager purchasers obstructed the swift darting of their progress, bringing them to a halt, and pennies clinked quickly in scabbed hands. '*Sensation ! Sudden Illness of Lord Mayor !*'

In the Guildhall, under the lights, the tables had looked magnificent. The note of peace, which had per-vaded and animated the Show, was carried right through the whole conception of the banquet, and great bunches of orchids, mauve and rose or spotted and stippled like snakes, were arranged in vases that were facsimiles of the most popular kinds of shell and bomb, but fashioned in gold plate. In the centre stood a golden skull, made into a loving cup ; a replica of the cranium of the executed chief of the enemy nation. This beautiful piece of work was a gift from the Mayors of the principal cities of our Allies. The guests had spilled turtle soup down their red, voracious gullets ; roast beef had fol-lowed, after soles ; sorbets, quails, ices, grapes in jewelled bunches, sweets, all had gone down the same scarlet path. Now came the toasts and, best of all, the speeches. The Prime Minister of the day stood up, to couple the name of the Lord Mayor with Peace and Democracy.

'The vast panorama of peace,' he had begun, 'which has been so ably, so ingeniously, translated for us into

terms of pageantry today, is indeed an inspiring, an —
em — er — almost an intimidating prospect. Across the
water, now, no enemy exists. World-famed empires
have been thrust down beneath the mire of the centuries,
and cities of a legendary renown and beauty have been
erased, or, in the more amiable term of one of our great
allies, liquidated. (Laughter.) This is an achievement
of which all who shared in it may well be proud. And
in it, no one has better played his part than the old, and
I am glad to say, the new (cries of hear, hear !) Lord
Mayor. You know him here, in this great City of
London — I know him, as he was to us, in his private
capacity during the hour of the nation's need. He is a
great killer ! (Tremendous applause.) The complicated
and wonderful killing machines, which his genius has
shaped, and his indomitable energy produced, are second
to none. Though it may be said — and it is high praise
— that in a world where every international effort has
seemed doomed to failure, the great armament firms
alone have set an example of successful co-operation, yet
he has shown himself a patriot, first and foremost, willing
to slaughter all who bar the nation's progress. But you
know him : you may well be proud of him ; I need
say no more, except that his example must inspire us.

'The ideals of Europe, those ideals of Christianity,
of brotherly love and chivalry, which raised the great
cathedrals, have seldom been better exemplified than in
the laying low of these same edifices. Our ideals have
won through, and we stand on the threshold of a new

world. It is in many ways, in most ways, a far, far better world than the old ; but it will not be — oh no ! — an easy world. But I have never promised you easy things. In the old days, after we had fought, we lived by trade ; but now the extermination of our chief customers has rendered us independent of them. Instead we must live by insuring each other's washing, which we must increasingly take in. But, Your Royal Highnesses, Your Excellencies, my lords, ladies and gentlemen, what is the lesson — the lesson that we must learn and treasure in our hearts, if not in our heads, from henceforth ? (Pause.) That we must be true to ourselves (outburst of stamping) — to ourselves, I was saying ; that we must steel our hearts, in the sacred cause of Equality and Free Speech, to kill everyone who does not agree with us (prolonged cheering), so that another war may be unthinkable, and so that men, pacific at heart as the beasts of the field, the forest and the jungle, may enjoy in peace those blessings which they deserve. But we are not revengeful — oh no ! Nor, as I can prove, are we selfish. For a war, out of which we gain no material advantage, must be as unselfish and praiseworthy as, judged by the standard of statesmanship, it is wise. The Little Man, now master, entered the last war from no motive of the head, but of the heart. And feeling is a more noble process than thinking — and more democratic : for everyone can feel, but not everybody can think (cheers). Otherwise I should not be addressing you here today, for there are sterner tasks to which I should attend. In the

Peace before you, I offer you no period of slothful ease
(cheers), no time for talk or reflection (stamping). It
must be an epoch of endeavour, of strife (tremendous
applause), of sweat (roars and cheering), of keeping your
nose to the grindstone (tumultuous cheers, and waving
of handkerchiefs) : it must be . . .' And in this manner
the great oration tottered inexorably to its appointed
anticlimax.

Then, after it had ended, and after the storm of cheering had subsided, the toastmaster knocked again on the
table with his gavel, and called out in a ceremonial
voice, tinged with its accustomed burden of superiority :

'Your Royal Highnesses, Your Excellencies, my lords,
ladies and gentlemen, pray silence for the Lord Mayor
elect of the City of London, now entering on his third
term of office : Sir Richard Whittington ! ! !'

The new Lord Mayor, his own successor, stood up,
and with a singular ease of manner and appearance of
spontaneity began his speech. All that day he had felt
ill, but no one would have known it : nor could he
himself make out quite what was the matter, suffering,
as he did, some uneasy stirring of the heart for which,
perhaps, modern doctors have not yet found a name.
As when a serious illness begins, so everything seemed
strange, and the senses, each one, sight, taste, smell,
hearing and touch, seemed to translate the messages they
received differently from their wont — especially hearing.
Even the pealing of the chimes of bells, now ringing to
announce his third span, carried for him an echo difficult

to seize, some refrain of words heard long ago.   At times
he almost caught their drift.   '*Turn again*', he thought
he could distinguish — but it must have been very long
ago.   Meanwhile, he was making his speech, and so
could not give full attention to the other matter.   And
he was speaking well.   ('*Turn again !*')

People liked to hear what he was saying, and Lady
Whittington, from the end of the table, was watching
him intently.   Dressed in black velvet, it was the emerald
ring she wore on her finger that first drew one's attention
— and no wonder, for it was the Whittington Emerald,
as it is called, one of the largest, and of the most pure
and vivid quality in the world.   (It had been acquired
for Sir Richard many years before in Tongador.)   But,
in any case, with her white hair, and her skin like white
kid, she was a handsome woman, especially at first sight.
It was as though she had been specially created to glow
with a white radiance at public functions, the whiteness
being there to show off the jewels, as the hoar-frost on a
Christmas tree is designed to set off the toys and tinsel.
But then, after having just accepted this conclusion, one
realised that, after all, the rime was genuine, thrown off
by the inner core, rather than the deposit of the years.
For so tall, imposing a person, she was well finished,
except for her hands, which looked like a sketch for
hands, curiously lumpy, too, so that when she took off
her long, fawn-coloured gloves it was as though she
were peeling potatoes.   With her large eyes, earth-
brown, she continued to scan her husband's face, and in

them shone a certain anxiety ; no doubt she knew that he had been feeling ill.

He spoke admirably ; a full ten minutes passed before he came to his chief theme, the gratitude that the nation, the Empire, the world, and those of the conquered even more than of the conquering powers, owed to the man who had just spoken. 'Gratitude,' he was saying, 'is perhaps the first, the most typical and important of human qualities, and it is one that the Little Man possesses in the lowest — I use "lowest" in its new democratic sense, meaning "highest" (a word that itself reeks of the prejudices of the bad old days) — in the lowest degree. The good faith of the crowd — and what is the crowd but a herd — I mean an august assemblage — of Little Men?—has long been proverbial as that of princes. But gratitude must not only be felt, it must be expressed, expressed for a lifetime. And how can this quality, this gratitude, best be expressed ?' . . . Here Sir Richard fell silent, to mark the end of one of the periods of his speech, no less than to allow a time for the burst of applause which this sonorous display of sentiment naturally promoted, partly to spend itself. As it began to die, he lifted up a hand in the style of the great orators to quell it. A profound silence of anticipation interposed, in which sounded a faint, sad mewing. Lady Whittington heard it, and looked over her shoulder. Her husband meanwhile was proceeding with his speech. 'Gratitude,' he was saying, 'gratitude —' but at this moment a gaunt, hungry-looking, rather mangy black cat, with wild and haunted eyes, jumped on to the table and turned its whiskered, grizzled face towards him.

The cat stole the limelight. On it the gaze of every guest was now fixed, as it stalked towards the Lord Mayor, so delicately threading its way among the orchids and gold plate. It was not, perhaps, really so unusual a cat, nor so old in its aspect as one might have presumed. It was not so much unlike the ordinary run — if one may use the word in that connection — of cats ; it even resembled many cats that can be seen flickering in figures-of-eight through railings, or leaping vertically, with the dynamism of ecstasy, up tree trunks, or up high walls to the beloved roof-tops, their dominion of the night. Nevertheless, when you looked, the cat *was* old, ancient more than old. . . . Now it had come so near the Lord Mayor that it rubbed its neck against his hand. 'Gratitude', he stammered with pale lips, 'gratitude' . . . and then, with a moan, fell back. The cat, seeming much concerned, jumped with grace and agility — considering its age — on to the floor, and nestled against him. The mewing turned to a loud contented purr. . . . Along the tables there was an uneasy stirring of hands and eyes, and a few guests, with less restraint than their fellows, murmured, 'So it *is* true. The man's haunted by a cat !' . . . The Lord Mayor was carried out into the air, Lady Whittington followed him and the guests dispersed.

For several days he was confined to his bed, and could see no one. But since the incident had aroused public interest, Lady Whittington allowed herself to be interviewed by members of the Press. She began, with considerable charm, to explain that Sir Richard was, and always had been — *always* was the word upon which she lingered — particularly devoted to animals, though she must confess that he preferred dogs to cats. His Sealyham, 'Tufts', was his constant companion, and she had often heard Sir Richard say that he did not know how he would have got through the war without the doggies. But, though he favoured dogs, he had done more for cats than any man living. He had founded first *The Whittington Central Cats' Aid Society and Sanatorium* : a place to which old cats could retire in comfort, where they could be well looked after, watched and tended, not allowed to stray, and where they could be sure, too, of their saucer of milk at regular intervals. But though this rest-house served, and continued to serve, a useful purpose, it was situated in too noisy and central a district to obtain the best results. It was very tempting for cats. So Sir Richard had then planned and endowed *The Cats' Charterhouse*, in the grounds of Whittington, the family seat in Gloucestershire, and finally, since that, too, failed to meet the need, he had inaugurated *The Cats' Provident Society Almshouse* in the Outer Hebrides.

All this work, into which had gone so much forethought and imagination, he had achieved for cats, though, in this resembling many gallant and eminent men before him — Lord Roberts and Lord Kitchener for

— from Whittington in Derbyshire. It is a comfortable enough little place now. Trams clank down the road between lines of red council-houses, each with, in the window, for show, an identical china ornament, the realisation of some strange ideal or perhaps, as at Pompeii, an offering to the God of Plenty : either a slouching boy, dun-coloured, with hands in his pockets, or a curtseying, winsome, small girl, in a half-crinoline, of which she holds up the ends in thick hands. Feudalism here has plainly been put a stop to, for the squire's house is a lunatic asylum, and laughter — or, if not laughter, a howling very like it — sounds continually over the well-kept lawns from where the lunatics play happily their innocent games of 'Smash the Sane Man' and 'Hunt the Warder' under the starred syringa bushes and fat-leaved, toad-speckled laurels. The Rectory is to become a Youth Hostel, or even a Civic Centre, and loud-speakers will be erected for teaching compulsory crooning at every street corner. . . . But I forget my trade. Dick Whittington, I was about to say when this vision of a municipal paradise I have just described impinged upon my mind and cut across my story, was a foundling, dis-covered one winter's night on the moor, outside the village, then still a rustic, backward place. He was adopted by a blacksmith and his wife, who brought him up as if he were their own son, providing him with a comfortable home, warm both in hearth and heart. The winter he enjoyed especially, for in the long dark after-noons he was allowed to sit at the back of the smithy,

which resembled a cave, listening to the rhythmic clang-
ing of hammer on anvil and watching the sparks trace
their comet-like path across the rectangle of dark-blue
sky through the doorway. All his life he remembered
this, the smell of the hot iron and singed hoof, and the
hammering and stamping of horses.

He was only twelve years old, however, when a great
plague swept the country, carrying off the smith and his
wife, so that Dick found himself back where he started
in the bleak and misty darkness of Whittington Moor,
a broken, wintry wood that lay south of the village,
towards the big town of Chesterfield. At night the
wind roared through the scrubby young beech and
sycamore, and whistled through the chinks of the low,
loosely built walls of dun stone. With darkness, the boy
would fall asleep, but the cold wind would soon wake
him, and he would lie on his coat, spread on the ground,
watching the flames of Staveley Furnace, that moved like
the tongues of lions, or a few sparks that flew up from
the pyramid of cinders making a pattern against the sky.
And this would cause him to think again of his father,
rhythmically hammering, the sparks flying up from the
anvil until, as he lay there, he seemed almost to hear that
double sound, both sharp and bell-like. . . . There was
no one to look after him, and no one for him to look
after — except a small black kitten ; which, together with
a few things placed in a bandanna handkerchief, made
into a bundle and tied to his stick, formed his entire
possessions. It was not easy to feed the kitten, for she

o

Dogs, much more plainly than cats, have names attached to their personalities, because dogs are active, aggressive, belong to the business world and move much in military circles. (Almost every officer, young or old, is followed — or led — by a dog : but few are followed by cats.) So, for the most part, they bear the names of generals, though seldom of admirals or air marshals — and, of course, of the better kind of financier. (Down, Melchett ! Down, Joel !) Often, too, they are styled after politicians — (Down, Attlee, down, Selwyn — posterity is free to vary and modernise these labels) or bear imaginative onomatopoeic names that might, when uttered loudly, be the sound of their own barking : Spot ! Smut ! Shot ! Splash ! Dash ! Dingle ! But Dick found it difficult to know what to call the kitten, until one day a passing traveller, seeing her playing, asked him her name. Hearing that the lad had found none for her, he remarked : 'You ought to call her *Roxana* : it's a Persian name.' Liking its outlandish sound, Dick adopted the stranger's suggestion, shortening the word to *Roxy*.

One morning, in the pheasant-feathered tail of autumn, before the first snow had fallen, a crisp Derbyshire morning of cobwebs and mists and scented, golden bracken, and of red berries which — for there had been a gale — covered the path through the wood and scrunched underfoot, Dick and his kitten were setting out for London to seek their fortune. He felt sad at leaving, but the kitten stopped from time to time to play with a red berry on the green moss, knocking it backwards and forwards, and as Dick did not wish to waste time, he put Roxy in the pocket of his coat, with just her head showing out of it, and gradually her mewing and purring comforted him, until, whistling a popular tune of the day, *Three Sailor Lads*, he began to stride in the direction of Chesterfield confidently, almost cheerfully.

Already he could see the crooked, crumpled spire of the church there, round which, it was said, the devil had wound his tail, cork-screwing its shape in front of him ; but now he began to feel hungry, and called at a tall farmhouse, that seemed so isolated in its own world of the early morning, with its sounds of lowing and braying and cackling and clucking, as to be an hallucination that by midday would vanish with the fading mists ; but it proved to be substantial enough, and there he obtained a drink of milk for himself and his kitten. The farmer's wife told him, at the same time, to come to the kitchen fire and warm himself. Sitting by the fire was a carter who asked the boy what business he was on, and hearing his story, and that he was bent on going to London, where even the paving-stones, the lad had been told, were made of gold, said that he would give him a lift there. For three days they drove southward, and then, one morning, just as the winter's sun was topping the dome of St. Paul's, the good-natured carter put him down, before continuing on his way to Canterbury. Sure enough, Dick saw the gold lying in heaps and strips on the pavement ; but it could not be picked up. It was a singular morning, full of the tongues of bells, which were to play so important a part in his life, as well as of this delusive golden light.

It was not long, alas ! before Dick discovered how little gold was to be found — and even how little paving, except in the churchyards, where he slept of a night, above the bones of generations. The city *must* be very rich, he supposed, but there was little sign of it in the exteriors of the houses, and he never saw the inside of them, though a policeman had promised him he would see the inside of a prison. For the most part, people were so busy that when he tried to stop them to tell them his story, they merely hurried on. The carter, when he left, had given him a loaf, but that was three days ago, and for a whole day he had had nothing to eat, nor had poor Roxy, and no one had spoken to him, except the policeman of whom I have just told you, and an officer of the Society for the Prevention of Cruelty to Animals, who had come up to him, and had said that the kitten looked half-starved, and that if the boy was not careful he would be prosecuted. Hearing this, Dick ran off as fast as his weak legs would take him. . . . That night, in the churchyard, Roxy howled for the first time — hitherto, she had only mewed and purred — and this had given him an idea. The next day, he sang in the streets, holding his hat in front of him. . . . Fortunately, he sang very badly, and had a loud voice, so people listened and liked his singing, as always in London streets, and gave him money — and advice. 'Don't get your voice trained whatever you do,' they advised him, 'or you'll spoil its freshness.' Even now, however, he barely earned enough to keep himself and Roxy.

One morning Dick was singing outside a grand house in a square, when a large old gentleman, standing in a bow-window, heard him. The old gentleman remained there for a minute or two, puffing like a whale, in the way that large old gentlemen are apt to puff when they stand in bow-windows. Then he turned away, and in a moment or two had opened the door and had arrived in the open air, under the portico. From there, with a manner suggesting that he thought he could not be seen, he examined the boy, very slowly, very carefully, and when his eyes had reached as far as the kitten's black face, peering out of the pocket of the ill-fitting jacket, and her two white paws hanging over it from their joints, he began to walk ponderously down the steps. Dick went on singing. It was a rather dismal sound, he realised, but the feel of the cold, hard pavers of the churchyard was still in his young bones, nor had he been able to afford breakfast.

The old gentleman, advancing towards him, had said :

'The police'll be after you, m'lad, if you go on like that. Stop that horrible noise, can't you ?'

'Please, sir, I can't stop it,' Dick replied. 'I'm doing it for my living.'

'Well, tell me your story instead.'

This Dick proceeded to do, and having heard it, the

old gentleman pronounced : 'You shall have work in my house.'

'But I can't be separated from my cat,' Dick cried, pointing to his kitten.

'Certainly not,' the old gentleman agreed, 'you can't leave her. Besides she'll probably make a fine mouser. She has the look of one to me — and there's always room in the world for a mouser.'

Then the old gentleman took Dick into the hall, rang the bell, and when the butler answered it, said 'Grinder ! take this lad downstairs, and tell Mrs. Grinder that first, before anything else, she's to give him, and his kitten, some breakfast. . . . I'll see her later.'

Dick had noticed how different the old gentleman's clothes were from any that he had hitherto seen : for everything he wore appeared to be of the finest material, though most sober and plainly cut. And now it turned out that he was a famous merchant. He owned a fleet of ships, and traded with Russia for sables, for drugs of Tartary, and the white furs of the Arctic Circle — where, on occasion, his ships took so great risks for him, in going to the farthest extremity of the ocean, that they are still there, fast in the ice — with India for spices and pepper, with Arabia for perfumes, with Egypt for henna and kohl, with the rest of Africa for diamonds and emeralds, and with the races of the distant isles, who grow horse-hair on their heads, for pearls ; to all these places he sent in return English wool or English cloth. Mr. Fitzwarren — for that was the old gentleman's name

— was a widower with one daughter, Pamela, a lovely girl of ten, but rather large for her age ; indeed she was already taller than Dick by an inch or two. She had fair hair, of a darker colour than usual, brown eyes, and a thick, smooth, fair skin : but an unusual elegance attended her. She was very proud, though, and not as kind as her father, and thought it beneath her dignity even to look at Dick.

The task allotted to him in the house was to wait on Mrs. Grinder, and since he was in her company all day in the kitchen, or within reach in the scullery, she would always make use of every chance for finding fault with him. Indeed he was glad when night came, and he could go to bed ; for he had been given a garret to himself, right at the top of the house. This bare little room had one window, opening on to the roof, and so, very convenient for Roxy. In the morning he would have to get up at five to clear the stoke-hole and light the fires for boiler and kitchen. Mrs. Grinder would not come down till eight o'clock, and from that time on she would always find the opportunity to give Dick a harsh word or allot him an unpleasant task. For example, she would often order him to peel the onions, so that his eyes should water. Then she would laugh at him and call out 'Crybiby !' She was for ever telling him that she would poison his cat if the animal entered the kitchen (which she did constantly to look for Dick). And it appeared almost as if Roxy provoked Mrs. Grinder purposely, for the manner in which the cat, as she grew older, caught

mice almost in defiance of Mrs. Grinder, who maintained
that she herself was so clean and economical a cook that
there could be none in the house, must have infuriated
her. And Roxy, as if to emphasise their numbers, commonly carried the scalps of the mice to her master, laying
them out in a row on the kitchen floor, so that they could
be counted by anyone who walked through, and there
could be no gainsaying them. The cat brought them to
Dick either as a sign of her own prowess, or as a gift ;
but Mrs. Grinder thought it an act of mere spite, and
pretended to think that the cat caught them in neighbouring houses. She proceeded, therefore, to take it out of
Dick in a variety of ways. Herself, she talked Cockney,
and therefore liked to make fun of the boy's way of
talking, for he 'spoke broad', as the phrase goes in
Derbyshire. He used 'Tha' and 'Thee', and said
'yoursen' for 'yourselves', and indulged in many uncouth and rustic expressions. In her acrid voice Mrs.
Grinder would mimic him, for she liked to humiliate
him in front of people, especially in front of Miss Pamela,
since she loved the little girl as much as she hated Dick
and Roxy. He used to hide sometimes, so as to see the
child pass, and Mrs. Grinder, noticing this, would pretend
not to be aware of it, and then, as Miss Pamela went by,
would haul him out of his refuge, thereby making him
look silly. Or if the little girl chanced to stop for a
moment to play with Roxy — to whom she paid more
attention than to Dick, for cats are all of one class —
Mrs. Grinder would call her to order, saying, 'Now,

Miss Pamela, that dirty little animal belongs to that dirty little boy, and isn't for the likes of yaou to pli' with !'

Mrs. Grinder's friends alleged that she had a kind heart, and indeed it may be so, but a kind tongue would have been more to the purpose. Unfortunately, she prided herself on 'always speaking out, to people's fices'. With her, however, it took three, not two, to make a quarrel, for, besides the person whom she assaulted, she had to have another in whom she could confide her injuries and triumphs. Thus, when Mrs. Grinder was having one of her perpetual rows with other people, she would temporarily become more amiable to Dick ; but he hated her grumbling about others almost more than her direct abuse of himself.

She would usually stand with a chopper at the kitchen-table, her figure looking during these moods like an old-fashioned cottage loaf, her face fashioned, it seemed, of one of the raw meats with which she was always dealing. 'I knaow I've got a temper,' she would say to him, 'not one of those slaow tempers, Grinder mi' be thankful, but you knaow, easy to raouse, easy to gaow as they si' — but one thing I can't abide, and that's to let things gaow on and not speak aout. I can't bear false fices, or people 'oo si' one thing to your fice and another be'ind your back. I must 'ave it aout. Neither Grinder nor me are ones to let things lie on us ; oh, naow, not us. So I said to Grinder, "You gaow and fetch 'er, and I'll tell her strite, I will, to 'er fice." "I shouldn't," Grinder said, "I shouldn't, Mother ; you'll only upset yourself."

"I'm not a coward, Grinder," I said, "a runner ; I can
look arter myself if it comes to that !" So 'e brought
'er. . . . I didn't si' much, you knaow. I didn't let myself gaow ; I jus' said "Hemmer, yer mean, sneaky little
'aound, was it yaou that told Mrs. Norbury as I said
Mrs. Craowker was'n better than she should be ; was it
yaou, yaou dirty cringer, yaou, speaking one thing to the
fice, and another be'ind the back ? Was it yaou ? Aout
with it," I ses, like that, "Aout with it, for I like things
strite and above board. If I 'ave a thing agen a person,
then I si' it — but si' it abaout 'em, that's a thing I'd never
do. Never. Neither me nor Mr. Grinder, and if Mrs.
Craowker is naow better than she should be, what 'as
that to do with me ?" I ses. "That," she ses, very stuck
up and nasty, "is what I ask myself, Mrs. Grinder." "O
you 'orrible little beast," I ses, as quick as anything, "you
mean 'ound, so it was yaou ! I'd be ashimed to be
your mother, I would. Hemmer . . ." ' So the de-
nunciation, the repining, would continue, sometimes for
hour after hour.

At last, driven equally beyond endurance by her bad
treatment of him and her nagging confidences, he determined to run away. Yet he hesitated and procrastinated
because Mr. Fitzwarren had been so kind to him, and he
feared it might seem ungrateful, and, in addition, a single
amiable glance from Miss Pamela would make him alter
his mind. At last, however, one morning after breakfast, he overheard Mrs. Grinder — who was chopping
up a chicken at the time, and did not realise that he was

standing in the doorway — confide in a loud voice to
one of the kitchen-maids, 'I taold the Master that Dick
might mike a cabin-boy on one of his ships, but 'e'll
never mike a footman or even a pantry boy, so the
Master's only keeping 'im till the winter's aowver,
because it's difficult to find another boy naow, and then
'e's sending 'im to Japan.'

When Dick heard these words, they decided him —
since he had no means of telling that they were not true —
and he crept out of the house, stopping neither to pack
his bundle nor even to take his stick. He ran as fast as
he could, not troubling to look where he was going
(what did it matter ?) : but after about forty minutes
he became tired and pulled up. Besides, the morning
was beautiful — for that, though few people realised it,
was what it was — so beautiful that he stood still and,
as he did so, had the sense of something tremendously
important about to happen to him. . . . It was eleven
o'clock on a February morning, and the winter crispness,
just touched with spring, lingered in the air, while the
sun was spreading its miser's gold along the pavement.
And though coal, which adds its dark substance to
the native mists of London and turns them into fogs,
was burning in many thousands of open grates, yet
in the air there was only a vaporous opalescence that
wrapped itself like a fleece round the sun and, seemingly,
a fragrance of wood-smoke, as though it had been
blown into the great city from many hamlets on the
edge of forests.

In the deserted, paved space where Dick now found himself, there was no one passing, no one hurrying. It was a neglected corner, full of the feeling of other days. Nothing stirred. . . . A hush prevailed, as if sound were dead and with it the power of hearing : albeit this loss appeared to strengthen other senses. He tried, under these influences, to sum up for himself what he felt, and why he had this so urgent intimation, derived from the very air, of something momentous for him : but all that he could decide was that he felt lonely. . . . And just then he heard a loud contented purring, and looking down, saw Roxy scampering upon velvet paws in the minute playground she had made for herself round his boots, for one of the laces had come undone and trailed on the pavement, and she was knocking the tag, and jumping after it, and performing a thousand pretty feats of simulation, so as to preserve in her animal mind the fiction that it too was a living thing.

Dick had forgotten the very existence of his cat, but now he took her up and stroked her, and, as he did so, a thing occurred which he was never to forget. As if he were watching a bud break into a perfection of flower, of which it was impossible even to dream, all the bells of London began to ring : bells old and bells new, hoarse bells and bells that were shrill, bells loud-mouthed and bells soft-singing, cracked bells and whole bells, bells that talked of material affairs and bells that sang of ideals lost or realised, bells that wheezed and bells that whispered, tolling bells and pealing bells, bells that spoke with the voice of angels and bells that sang from depths to a darker vision. The air itself seemed to be of the substance of their vibration. In after years he wondered whether it really could have happened, and what it could have portended, what it signified : for, indeed, there were no victories to celebrate except those always current in a great city, the victory of greed over kindness, age over youth, Dives over Lazarus, the healthy over the sick. But why should bells ring for such ordinary triumphs of a metropolis? . . . Still, they *had* rung.

They rang for a full ten minutes, carillons of frost and sun, songs that with the greatest virtuosity sang an idiot tune. Then, suddenly, they changed in an instant, and just as, when you are in a railway carriage, the train can fit its rhythm to anything, sing in your ear any words or composition it chooses, from a Beethoven symphony to a song such as 'I do like to be beside the seaside', so all at once the bells sang in unison these words :

> *' Turn again, Whittington,*
> *Lord Mayor of London !*
> *Turn again, Whittington,*
> *You must be bold.*
> *Turn again, turn again !*
> *Learn again, learn again !*
> *Then London will bring you*
> *Your streets paved with gold.'*

On hearing this message, so strangely delivered, Dick returned to Mr. Fitzwarren's house, and when his master sent for him, and enquired why he had run away, the

air of expectancy obtained. The most thrifty of the
household brought money to Mr. Fitzwarren to invest in
the enterprise, but the rest of them brought their most
precious possessions : for example, housemaids and
kitchen-maids brought such things as a filigree box, sent
from India by a sailor-cousin; a pincushion in puce velvet
with *Dinna Ken*, or some Scottish motto of that sort,
inscribed on it in false seed pearls; a turquoise brooch
consisting of a spider's bulbous body caught in its own
web of golden threads — or were they legs ? — ; a match-
box of Dutch silver, with a pattern on the top that human
eye could never unravel; a china figure, of matt surface,
but eruptive, that represented an idealisation of 1880
charm, all flounces, smiles and frills ; an alarum clock of
some grievous white metal, through which showed a
yellow core, its bell worn at the jaunty angle to which
the years had knocked it ; a china box with a fox-terrier
painted on it, the poor little creature's head very much
on one side, as though a stroke had interposed, giving to
a mood of intense and foolish inquisitiveness a temporary
permanence ; a silver photograph frame, embossed with a
design of tulips ; and a cushion, black silk one side, and
white on the other, with painted on it in water-colour a
vivid, realistic design of red poppies. Everyone brought
something, money or personal chattels, all except Dick.
Alone of the whole household he had no savings and no
belongings with which he could part. Thus, while the
others were talking cheerfully of what the vessel would
bring them on the return voyage, Dick, dispirited and

humiliated, would sit in his garret, with his cat for sole company.

His idea came to him only just in time. One afternoon, as the household gathered on the steps to give a send-off to the Captain, who had been having luncheon with his employer, and was now starting to go down to the docks, Dick, who was at the back, broke through the little knot of people, with Roxy asleep in his arms, and cried to Mr. Fitzwarren :

'I have nothing of my own, sir, nothing to sell, except this cat. She is all I have to make my fortune. Please take her, sir, and ask the Captain to sell her for me.'

At this the cat — she was now full grown, though of slight stature — struggled to escape ; but her master handed her over to Mr. Fitzwarren, and he passed her on to the Captain. She now remained still and quiet, but, sitting up on the Captain's arms, gazed at Dick, while two large tears, that glittered like diamonds (but they were *not* diamonds or Roxy would have been retained at home), formed in her eyes. It was, indeed, an affecting scene, and much impressed all those who were there, even Mrs. Grinder. Miss Pamela cried, while her father warmly congratulated the boy on his spirit of enterprise, and above all, of self-sacrifice. And a Mr. MacMagnus, a close friend of Mr. Fitzwarren, and a master of industry, who had also been present at the luncheon, exclaimed, so that everyone could hear it, 'That young man will go far.' Since Mr. MacMagnus possessed a

P

reputation for spotting coming men, these words produced all the more effect.

The Captain, still clasping Roxy in his arms, climbed
into the waiting cab, and as it drove away, the master
of the house, Miss Pamela, Mr. MacMagnus and the
cluster of servants waved their hands and cheered. Roxy
still made no effort to escape, but even above the rattling
of the wheels and the cheering could be heard her
sobbing. But it did not reach Dick, for in his head
rang bells that sang :

> *'Turn again, turn again !*
> *Learn again, learn again !'*

Time began to move more quickly, for Dick was
growing up. He was much more popular in the house
now. For one thing, it was generally felt that his giving
the cat away like that showed that there was something
to him, and proved that he possessed both character and
acumen. And, in itself, the absence of the cat made life
easier for him. Mrs. Grinder, for example, no longer
bore him a grudge, had even come to like him. And
everyone in the house seemed now to value his society
because of his cheerfulness, for the truth was that in the
two years that had elapsed since Mr. Fitzwarren had
last heard of his ship, the whole household had grown
depressed : for them, so much was at stake.

At last a message reached Mr. Fitzwarren that the
vessel was still lying loaded in the harbour of Nebaka-
Koko, the chief port of Tongador, and, worse, that a
great plague was sweeping over the country. Many

began to fear that the Captain and his crew were dead, and that, in consequence, they would lose or had lost all they possessed — but Dick had only lost his cat, if that were so, and he thought little about the matter.

It must have been two or three years after the ship had left England, when Dick had almost reached manhood, that one night — he still slept in the garret — he woke up with a start. A full moon shone through the open window, showing a world of roofs. He thought the cold must have woken him, for it was a very frosty night, but then he heard a mewing, and, with a tremendous bound, a black cat leapt lithely across the sill and landed on his bed. . . . Well, it was odd, though there was nothing particularly surprising in it, he supposed ; but as the animal raised her body, the moon caught it, and he saw that this particular cat fairly blazed with jewels — which *was* a little surprising. At first Dick thought he must be dreaming. The cat stood, arching its back, in a flood of light from the moon. A small dog-collar of enormous brilliants surrounded its throat, though the long, silky Persian hair a little obscured their scintillation. What appeared to be a single huge emerald sparkled from the left ear, being inset there after the Hindu fashion, and round the right forepaw glittered an anklet of rubies. But this could be no dream, for the cat came straight to Dick, and, as he sat up in bed, jumped on his shoulder, and rubbed its head against his neck.

It *was* Roxy, there could be no doubt about it. She

purred loudly, and after a few minutes climbed down
from Dick's shoulder on to the bed, and sat there, looking
at him, and scratching at her neck with a paw, as if she
wanted something. After a while Dick understood : she
wanted him to undo the clasp for her and take the necklace off. That done, the cat stretched herself beside him,
and slept.

The next day, the Captain, who proved to have survived all the dangers of the voyage, came to luncheon,
and afterwards sent for Dick, to tell him of his good
fortune, and how it happened.

When the ship had arrived at Nebaka-Koko, the great
plague was at its height. The negroes called it *The White
Death*. Everything was deserted ; every being, every
living thing in some of the vast, teeming cities, seemed
to be dead. As the ship approached the harbour, through
the atmosphere of the shore, where the torrid African
heat danced in a sultry confusion above beach and houses
and grounds, the crew had been amazed to see no bathers,
no boatmen, no loungers, no longshoremen even — only
an army of skeletons that balefully glittered. The fever
and heat had driven whole crowds down to the sea, to
try and cool their simmering blood. Some had died as
they entered the water, others where they stood or
reclined, under the vultures hovering above and considering how and when they might descend to enforce
equality, to prove that the black races, too, possessed the
whitest of skeletons. So this great multitude of the dead
reposed among the enormous shells, thick-lipped shapes

in nacre that are to be found on tropical shores, or stood out against a background of gardens, or trellised arbours and arches in the Moorish manner, and colonnades round which twisted the serpentine branches of the unfamiliar plants of the country, now expanding their huge orange and purple cups. The few black faces that remained from the plague seemed to have a green shutter of fear over them ; their eyes peeped out from the arches, rolling, as if in search of comfort. Even the whites of the eyes now had this green light in them.

Nor had it been any better in Ta-Balu, the capital, the great city. Few of the inhabitants dared to venture out of their houses, though the gaily coloured streets of mud and the chattering market-places were silent, shuddering in the white blaze of noon. Here and there a venomous serpent, escaped from the snake-charmers who had fallen dead in the chief piazza during the climax of their most ingenious tricks, hissed from a gutter, and the lions, now free of keepers, could be seen shaking their manes and trotting back with heraldic gait to their homes in the Central Forest.

Even now, though so many had already perished, the plague had increased in virulence. Day by day, those still living fell dead, as they walked, were carried in litters, or drove ; at the sides of the roads, in the ditches, the corpses lay, piled up, where they had tumbled as they contracted the sickness. And then it approached the precincts of *Mon Repos*, the Mountain Palace, where the Emperor, crowned and wearing his robes of State, and clasping the two-edged Sword of Justice in his hand, sat trembling in the innermost court. The corridors and galleries with their vast arches open to snare the winds, though usually full of courtiers and officials, were now empty : those who remained alive no longer wished to walk there, to catch the tainted air. Besides, superstition held — and science supported it — that the plague was borne by rats, and His Majesty himself had heard the sound of them, that increased noticeably from day to day in the galleries as he walked. And sometimes, when the Emperor felt so fearful of the creatures that he climbed to the top of the great tower, where, surely, he would be secure from them, even there, as he looked down on the enormous glistening expanse of the African champaign, with its groves of oranges that held under their leaves a perpetual night, dark and balmy, that was lit only by their fruit, with its hedges of pomegranate and its fields of mangoes and melons and paw-paws, he would see the furrows filled with an advancing army of horrid black shapes, all, it seemed to him, hurrying towards the Palace. What could he do ?

First he sent for the witch of the white people, the Rodent Officer of the Agricultural Control Board, lately inaugurated through Geneva, by the White Powers. She was a fat American woman, who wore a green Rodent Officer's coat, and blue serge trousers, inappropriate to her structure. She had a lighted cigarette stub clipped to her upper lip all the time she worked or talked. Having surveyed *Mon Repos* and its grounds, she put down two powders, a white and a black, to destroy the rats. On it they throve, and their progeny pullulated. Evidently word of the delicacies she had provided spread quickly, for the rats seemed to double the size of their armies in a day, as well as to increase noticeably in stature. Next the Emperor summoned a witch-doctor from a far province of his empire : she arrived, clad in veils and cowrie-shells, anointed her enormous body with a special sacred unguent, and danced wildly in every chamber of the Palace. Still the rats survived, though she was executed. Then dried herbs were burnt; but still the rats poured in from all directions. Then the most sacred relics were fetched from Ta-Balu, in procession, to the beating of drums made of human skin. Yet the whole country, when seen from the Tower of the Sun, seemed to be moving — and moving centripetally, in one direction.

The Emperor was growing desperate. As he sat in state on his throne of gold in the Hall of the Royal Fetishes — a great apartment hung with countless Venetian mirrors, one above another, spread haphazard over the walls, the many recesses of which each contained the immense skeleton of a brass bedstead — it seemed to him that the palace was almost empty save for the rats. The mirrors and the polished brass balls of the bedsteads reflected nothing but his own royal countenance ; even the pages, in their scarlet liveries and white wigs, which made their faces look still more black, were fewer ; they had 'gone away' — for nobody must mention death to the

Emperor. His courtiers *went away*, they never died. The mirrors, then, showed endless vistas of other mirrors, of a dusty, fly-blown pomp. The sound characteristic of the Palace had become no longer the throbbing of drums, but the bumping and squeaking of rats.

From the Hall of the Royal Fetishes the Emperor issued a proclamation that promised a great fortune to any living thing that would destroy the rats. He waited : alas, no slightest diminution of the scuffling occurred — and then, one noon, as he was returning for luncheon from the Hall, through the Great Coronation Corridor of the Golden Wind, as it was called, he saw, laid out with military precision in a long row, stretching from the door to the first of the open arches, the bodies of 151 rats. After the preliminary and instinctive shudder that the sight evoked, the Emperor was, of course, highly delighted. He looked everywhere around him, to see who was responsible for the massacre, but there seemed to be no one present — then, as his eyes searched every possible corner, to his surprise he observed a black cat leap out from hiding, and race along the gallery, until like a tiger it pounced on another black body. Soon the little cat, for it was not a large animal, returned down the middle of the corridor, and boldly placed at His Majesty's feet the burden it was dragging along, a big black rat, hardly smaller than itself. The Emperor, much impressed, clapped his hands, and ordered a bowl of zebra's milk to be brought immediately, so that the cat, his champion, should be able to recruit its strength

— and before many weeks had passed, Roxana — for it was she — had killed or driven out by intimidation every rat from the Palace, from the mountain, and from the surrounding plain. In consequence, the plague abated.

It had happened in this way : Mr. Fitzwarren had charged the Captain of his vessel to deliver in person a present to the Emperor, together with a letter. Finding, when he arrived at Nebaka-Koko, that the Court had already left Ta-Balu for *Mon Repos*, accordingly he rode on in that direction, taking the cat with him. Once Roxy had seen a rat, there was no holding her ; her fortune was made — and made it certainly was. For not only did the Emperor decree that a temple was to be built to her, not only did he confer on her the title *Lion Champion and Court Sacred Whisker*, but he bestowed upon her a sack filled with uncut jewels of great value. In addition, he ordered a large emerald to be cut for her ear, and a few weeks later gave an audience — it was safe now to receive people in the Palace — to all the foreign ambassadors and native dukes, and in front of them, as a mark of the imperial favour, had himself clasped the diamond dog-collar round the cat's neck, while the band of the Assassin Guard, dressed in their ceremonial uniform of leopard skins, and high open-work crowns made of human ribs, thumped and brayed in unison a march by Sousa. And further, as final proof of his pleasure, and in order to ensure Roxana's comfort in the future, the Emperor, after enquiring the name of her English master, despatched to 'Mr. Whittington' as

Roxy out to Tongador. The country had completely recovered its customary prosperity, and Dick and his cat were immensely fêted in whatever part of the Empire they travelled. They spent several happy months in *Mon Repos*, and Roxy was very contented on the whole, for she was nearly always in the company of her master. She would sit at his side for hours, by one of the open arches of the Great Coronation Corridor, where first she had made his fortune, watching the birds dip and swing over the brooding summer plain, carolling and turning as if to tempt her. Only then would she become a little restless, making a curious deep sound, mingled of fury and calculation, in her throat, while she measured with cocked eye the distance between her and the spire of the nearest cypress, which, though its scent was wafted so strongly thither, could not be attained. And again, now that there were no rats to hunt in the Palace, she missed the regular exercise; so evidently that, since the Emperor had appointed to the cat her own slaves, they would occasionally arrange a hunt for her for the day in some outlying portion of the royal domain. Even for these pleasures, she disliked — and showed it plainly — having to be parted from her master, albeit for so short a time.

Fortunately during these expeditions Dick was at no loss to find employment : for business constituted his chief interest, and he had brought it with him. Because Mr. MacMagnus had found an opportunity of speaking to him before he left, and had said :

'You know, my boy, I have your interests at heart.

They're very backward out there, where you're going.
. . . Now, don't say a word about it to dear old Fitz,
he's a dear old fellow, though so antiquated in his ways,
but take out some models of good modern stuff to show
the Emperor ; you know, the things that make modern
countries, and make them great — Bren guns, tanks,
flame-throwers. He's sure to be interested. I'll supply the
models, and if you are successful, I will make it worth
your while.' . . . When the Emperor saw the toys, he
was, naturally, delighted and ordered a great many of
the originals of each model from Mr. MacMagnus. And
already, before Dick had left the country, he had been
able to see for himself some of the benefits resulting
from his enterprise : for the Emperor had no sooner
obtained the articles — and they, together with the bills,
had been delivered with a praiseworthy promptitude —
than, in order to pay for them, he declared war on the
neighbouring State of Kobalola. It was rather difficult
to do, because the moral reasons for a war had to be
thought out quickly, and the Emperor, being an absolute
monarch, had to carry out this difficult work for himself.
However, he soon issued a moving proclamation :

'Our patience', it read, 'is exhausted. We have long
had no aim except to live in peace, only with that purpose in view has our great and unconquerable army been
built up. This power we never dreamt of using, until the
atrocities of the enemy, committed upon our allies, the
Race of the South, compelled us to submit our cause
to the dread arbitrament of war. We shall proceed

resolutely and unflinchingly towards our goal, to widen the world basis of Democracy, and institute a reign of peace in Kobalola.'

It can be imagined with what a burst of cheering the people of Tongador welcomed the inspiring sentiment and close reasoning of this document. The warriors fought with more than their accustomed bravery, and before many days had elapsed the Emperor had entered the enemy capital. Here Dick and Roxy joined His Majesty, in order to be present at the ceremonies that marked the Peace Treaty. This exacted a large indemnity — or tribute, as it used to be called — from the defeated power. And Dick, being, as Mr. MacMagnus had comprehended, an enterprising young man, was able to book a larger order from the ruler of it, for machines similar to those employed by the Emperor, but of an improved type.

When Dick returned to London, Mr. MacMagnus was delighted at the manner in which someone so new to business had carried out the suggested transactions. Moreover, divining the real nature of the young man's genius, he now proposed that, while Dick should remain a further two years with Mr. Fitzwarren so as to learn the details of the business, some of which, it appeared, were secret, he should, at the end of that period, leave him. Mr. MacMagnus would, in the meantime, found two new concerns, one connected with the making of armaments, the other of the same kind as Mr. Fitzwarren's,

and on Dick joining him, and bringing him the benefit
of his experience, he would be made a partner in both.
Dick, who, as he used to say, was determined 'to be
beholden to nobody', felt that this was an offer he could
not afford to refuse — besides, he wished soon to be in a
position to propose marriage to Pamela, with whom he
was more than ever in love, and he certainly could not
expect her to throw herself away. . . . For the present,
Mr. MacMagnus and Dick both agreed that it would
be better to say nothing of their plans, for fear of
competition.

Things now began to prosper with Dick, and this
state itself helped to intensify his run of fortune. Everyone agreed how much he had improved. He had quite
shed his old roughness, both of speech and conduct, and
was a typical young business man, as smart in his appearance as in the bargains he struck. It would have been
difficult to tell that he was not a Londoner bred. Mrs.
Grinder now always addressed him as 'Sir', when she
saw him, and consulted him, rather than Mr. Fitzwarren,
about her own small affairs. As for Pamela, she had
begun to return his affection, and Mrs. Grinder now did
everything she could to further the match. At the end
of two years, when, as arranged with Mr. MacMagnus,
Dick picked a quarrel with Mr. Fitzwarren and walked
out of the office, Pamela took the part of the young man.
Her father was very angry with him at first, but then, as
Mrs. Grinder said to Pamela, 'You won't mind my siying
it, Miss Pamela, but 'e's getting past it. Hit's time 'e

retired.' And, indeed, his luck had deserted him, and he had lost much money. On the whole, the world took Dick's side. Indeed, they thought him still further improved. And, before long Dick bought a house of his own — it happened to be the same mansion in which Mr. Fitzwarren had lived in the days of his prosperity.

The cat still followed Dick everywhere. At his wedding, when he married Pamela, Roxana followed him up the aisle, though she had been locked up in a room at home. Whenever he went to dinner-parties, she had to be locked up, to prevent her escaping, and then hiding outside, or, if possible, entering the house of his hostess, there lurking unobtrusively in a corner, until the moment came when she could safely make an effective sortie, leaping up on to the middle of the dinner-table. He was, of course, still very much attached to her — they were such old companions — but he could not help feeling a little ashamed on these occasions. Not, he had to admit to himself, that she ever upset anything when she jumped. No, it was not that. 'But after all,' as he remarked to Pamela one day, 'I mean to say, one doesn't want a cat dogging one's footsteps all the time — if it were a *dog*, it would be different.'

Pamela agreed with him. 'You can't let it go on for ever,' she advised. 'Some time you'll *have* to put a stop to it, and force her to stay at home.'

In fact, though Dick had never been at a public school, his feelings resembled those of a boy, upon some local occasion of festivity, shocked by the non-conformity of his parents' clothes or conduct. Worse still, the sight of the cat revived old stories. And though Dick was proud of having made his own way — and never ceased to say so — neither he nor Pamela liked to be reminded of it by others. They preferred to administer it as a shock, themselves, to those whom they met — and, in any case, what had the cat got to do with it?

Yet, though Dick began to dread Roxy's sudden emergence, there was, he had to admit to himself, nothing unusual now in the cat's appearance. If she would only stay there and watch him, instead of claiming his acquaintance so openly, not much harm would be done. Nobody would notice. She merely looked a rather old cat — she had begun to age. He had long ago removed the diamonds and rubies — not because they struck an *outré* note (though, indeed, they did), but in case any thief should see them, and trap and kill the cat for their value. They were now in safe custody in the bank in his own name. The emerald was the last jewel the cat retained, but about the time that Pamela became engaged to him, she had pointed out that the emerald, by its weight, might damage the cat's ear.

'What a lovely ring it would make!' she had added, no doubt hardly thinking of what she was saying.

The engagement was not a long one, for Mr. Fitz-warren had lost his fortune owing to increased competition in his business, and Pamela did not wish to be a burden on him. All his flair for his work seemed to have deserted him, and he had grown into a very old man.

At the same time she hardly liked, when she married, to leave him to look after himself, so she gave him a flat in Dick's house. It was so convenient for him — he knew the place so well — and yet this was the part of it he had known least, so he wouldn't grow tired of it. There were practically no stairs, and servants today did not like stairs — or basements (not that he had any servants, but still it made it more modern, convenient, and 'homey'), and so Pamela had suggested that the basement should be made into a separate flat for him, all of his own. The old gentleman seemed happy there ; at any rate he troubled no one — and everyone agreed what a thoughtful, considerate daughter he had. He was lucky — not every daughter was like that nowadays. And when Pamela and Dick went out of an evening to dine, or to the play, it was pleasant for them to know that they could leave the cat with someone they could trust. Indeed, Mr. Fitzwarren liked having the little creature with him, for he seldom went out or saw anyone. Even Mr. MacMagnus, when he came to dine with the young people upstairs, used to declare that it would make him too sad to see Mr. Fitzwarren as he was now, he'd been so different in the dear old days — still, of course, he'd go down at once and see him if it would do him any good or help him, but it wouldn't ! The old gentleman, on the occasion when Mr. MacMagnus — who was only three years younger — had gone to visit him, had hardly seemed to recognise his old friend, and was very glum. It would only unsettle him again, they agreed.

Q

later on. But I don't like to give her away. I don't know why.'

'It's all very well for you. You don't hear the talk. It's not nice for me — people bring out the whole story of your coming to London, and say that I've married beneath me. And that I know that I have done so doesn't make it any better !'

'Darling, please don't say such hard things !'

'But you oughtn't to put up with it. You ought to show more respect for your wife. . . . Besides, it would be kinder to the cat herself.'

'She looks quite well — though we hardly ever see her, really, do we ?'

'You should send her right away — otherwise it'll be the same thing all over again. You don't see the sort of stir that goes round when she appears. You complain that it makes *you* look a fool, but what about me ?'

'I didn't say so, darling : you said it.'

'Please don't interrupt and contradict me, Dick, when we're talking of serious matters.'

At the moment, though, Pamela saw she could accomplish nothing. It was better to wait. So she put up with the cat until one day it got upstairs, into the drawing-room, and hid there. Some friends had come to see her, and after tea they asked her to play the piano to them. She had begun to give them her favourite Chopin Prelude, and was almost in the middle of it, when Roxy, from her place of concealment, howled in so loud, piercing and heartrending a tone, that Pamela had been obliged to stop. *That*, she realised, *had* made her look silly : it could not go on. . . . In short, not only was Roxy damaging Dick, she was a nuisance in the house and indeed everywhere.

Next time she approached the matter more softly, more obliquely.

'Darling,' she said to her husband one morning, 'Daddy's beginning to look such an old crock now, I'm sure country air is what he needs ! It would do him *so* much good, and after all he *is* my father ! So I've asked Tickle and Galbraith to look out for a cottage in Cornwall. It's such a wonderful climate, they say. . . . Only he mustn't be allowed to feel lonely at his age, so I thought we could send Roxy down too, to keep him company — then he'll be quite happy.'

As she had hoped, Dick fell in with this plan. . . . But the truth of the matter was, the cat was getting beyond herself. Even in the taxi on her way to the station, she scratched and roared inside her hamper like a tiger. In the station it was worse — and no sooner had she arrived than she was back again. How she made the distance from Cornwall to London in the time, it was impossible to imagine ! She hadn't arrived at the cottage till past midnight — but the very next evening, when Pamela and Dick had gone out to dine with Lord and Lady Nuggett (he was head of the great cartel which had recently been formed with the object of helping backward countries to become forward), there was a sudden commotion, and Roxy leapt like a steeplechaser over the extended arm of the footman, who was in the act of offering a gold platter to the chief guest, into the middle of the table, just in front of Dick. . . . Naturally, the story revived. Even Dick began to feel more strongly about Roxy's behaviour. One didn't want the whole thing to be raked up again.

Worse still, the cat proved to have become a thief. Usually Pamela wore the emerald ring, but one day, when she was not wearing it, and when the cat had come up to London secretly, Pamela, herself unseen, observed the animal deliberately go up to the jewel-box — which was unlocked — open it with teeth and paws, and then try to sneak off, carrying the wonderful gem in her mouth. When Pamela attempted to take it away, she fought like a fury. Fortunately, Dick was near, and directly he spoke to the cat, she gave it up quietly and lay on her back, as if she expected him to play with her.

The next day, Pamela, who had been for some time considering the whole matter of the cat, tried a new line of approach, and a new plan.

'Richard,' she said — she had begun to call him Richard by now, it was such a much nicer name, she thought, than Dick — 'Richard, you're so fond of cats, I wonder you don't start an almshouse for old cats. It would do so much good — and you're rich enough to afford it now. They've done a lot for you, you know, in your career : now it is up to you to do something for them. It would help to raise the whole status of the cat in society. And your cat, dear little Roxy — I've grown so fond of her — could be the first there, with a really good endowment policy. She's growing old now, and deserves to be properly looked after. I'm afraid she's not really happy with Daddy, down in Cornwall, or she'd stay down there, and not try so often to get away — and it shows, too, that he can't exercise proper supervision. Perhaps she'd be more contented in London again. And it will be easier for other cat-lovers if the home is built here. . . . And I've found such a nice capable man to organise everything. He's had a great deal of experience and is thoroughly reliable. . . . He was a warder at Dartmoor for a long time.'

The idea appealed to Dick. Within the space of a year, *The Whittington Central Cats' Aid Society and Sanatorium* — about which you asked me — was completed at great expense.

But, as Lady Whittington (Dick was now Sir Richard, having entered on his first term of office as Lord Mayor of London) pointed out, it would not be fair for him to have to find *all* the money for the charity, even though it had been his idea, and he was so wealthy now. He must remember that he had done it in honour of Roxy, and, after all, the cat was a rich cat. Luckily, for once he was prepared to listen to reason, and sold some of the animal's jewels to defray part of the cost of the home. . . . The details of it had been thought out with the greatest care, and one well could see why it had cost so much money. There was a proper staff of attendants provided, and each cat — but at first there was only one cat

at the Mansion House, Sir Richard would lie awake for hours. The fire burning in the grate would throw the shadows of the plumes that crowned the bed upon the wall; sometimes it would show palm trees, then the shadows would flutter and coalesce back into chaos, and re-form themselves, of a sudden, into the momentary likeness of a gigantic black cat, glaring at him. He would be wide awake again, and no sooner had he with the greatest difficulty at last got to sleep, than a gentle mewing would wake him — and there would be Roxy !
. . . It used to distress Lady Whittington even more, to think of the cat, at her age, out in the cold night like that ! And how she contrived her sudden disappearances from the home it was difficult to make out ; for windows and doors were shut and bolted, and a fire was kept burning — so she could not have got up the chimney. No attendants, no bribes of milk or mice, no iron bars, could keep her away from Sir Richard Whittington.

The Whittingtons now placed all their hopes in a new idea — in *The Cats' Charterhouse* that, at Lady Whittington's suggestion, Sir Richard had decided to found in Gloucestershire, in the grounds of his own country house, so that his wife could herself, from time to time, keep an eye on the place and see that the cats were comfortable. . . . But it was no use. The instant Dick came to London, Roxy appeared too, and so old and mangy now, so gaunt and prophetic in her look, that it was difficult to recognise in her the purring black kitten that once she had been. You could almost hear the animal's bones continued, 'it is due chiefly to ignorance. Even today few people, comparatively, speak French — and still fewer spoke it thirty years ago. But Sir Richard in his early days travelled a good deal and spoke French fluently. Talking it so well, he became fond of the language, and it was one of his ways as a young man, even when speaking English, to introduce frequently a French word or phrase. And so, when strangers used to ask him, "To what do you attribute your great success ?" my husband has often, in my hearing, answered, "In the first place to *achat*" — or, in plain English, "to purchases". These people, knowing no French, and consequently misunderstanding what he said, would go away and tell their friends "Whittington himself told me he owed his fortune to a *chat*, or cat." In a similar fashion, certain persons eager for sensation, and ready to seize on any evidence for the manufacture of a story — and you gentlemen of the Press know that such persons can always be found — have twisted to their purpose something else my husband used to say. In the course of building up the great industry that my husband and Lord MacMagnus founded, it was necessary for the firm to acquire its own mines, round Newcastle in point of fact, and to have its own fleet of ships to bring the coal south. For this purpose, my husband found the most convenient vessel to be a Norwegian type called in that language, a *cat*. Accordingly the ships of this fleet were called cats. And often, when I've visited Sir Richard at the works, I've heard him make some remark like this :

"I've been waiting for my cat all day," or "I can't think what we should do without our cat!" . . . *Those* are the cats of which you talk! And in the same way, there's that stupid tale of a cat having brought him a fortune from the negroes! That is due to the sailors on the colliers having black faces from the coal dust. . . . Except the cats of which I've told you, I know of no cat in my husband's life.'

Just as she said this, while the words were still on her lips, a scratching sounded at the door of the room, and the journalist I have already had cause to mention opened it before Lady Whittington could stop him. A cat — plainly the same that had been seen previously at the Banquet — dashed in, looked round, and then fled out again, and up the stairs to her master's bedroom, where he lay, under his plumed canopy, more seriously ill than his wife realised.

He died a rich man. But it was found that by some strange freak, he had altered his will, only a few days before his death, and had left his whole enormous fortune to the maintenance of his various cats' homes. Lady Whittington had to part with her jewels, and passed the remaining years of her life in seclusion in her late father's cottage in Cornwall. She seemed, as she grew older, to become a very ordinary old lady, except that her neighbours noticed how fiercely, even though she was now rather infirm, she would shoo away any cat that strayed into the garden or attempted to enter the house.

As for Roxana, she was never seen again. Some say

she was poisoned, and that the Lord Mayor's State Bed-room at the Mansion House is haunted by her spectre, though others maintain that this loyal and gifted cat, after her master's decease, made her way back to the scene of her former splendours, ending her life in *Mon Repos* as the honoured guest of the Emperor.   But this second report does not seem to me altogether likely, for Sir Richard's great business capacity and enterprise had been responsible for supplying every kingdom in those regions with the most advanced weapons of modern warfare, and, by the time each of these countries had given the rest a New Order, and had then liberated one another, it is not to be supposed that many dwellings, many Emperors — or many subjects — were left. . . . And the most glorious war of all, the Crusade for the Lowest Common Denominator, was still to come.   But, at least, it has been stated in the last few weeks by reput-able travellers that the Temple the Emperor raised to Roxana still stands unscathed in the remote mountains of Tongador.

THE END

PRINTED BY R. & R. CLARK, LTD., EDINBURGH